Kafka's Hat

Patrice Martin

Translated by Chantal Bilodeau

To Colleen
Enjoy!
P. [illegible]
June 2013

Hat

k a ’ s

Talonbooks

Talonbooks
P.O. Box 2076
Vancouver, British Columbia, Canada V6B 3S3
www.talonbooks.com

Typeset in Arno and printed and bound in Canada
Printed on 100% post-consumer recycled paper
Cover and interior design by Typesmith

First printing: 2013

The publisher gratefully acknowledges the financial support of the Canada Council for the Arts, the Government of Canada through the Canada Book Fund and the Province of British Columbia through the British Columbia Arts Council and the Book Publishing Tax Credit for our publishing activities.

Le chapeau de Kafka by Patrice Martin was first published in French in 2008 by Éditions XYZ. We acknowledge the financial support of the Government of Canada, through the National Translation Program for Book Publishing, for our publishing activities.

Library and Archives Canada Cataloguing in Publication

Martin, Patrice, 1963–
Kafka's hat / Patrice Martin ; translated by Chantal Bilodeau.

Translation of: Le chapeau de Kafka.
Issued also in electronic format.
ISBN 978-0-88922-743-9

I. Bilodeau, Chantal, 1968– II. Title.

PS8626.A7728C4213 2013 C843'.6 C2013-900152-2

To Michaela and Madeleine

When reading Kafka, I cannot avoid approving or rejecting the legitimacy of the adjective "Kafkaesque," which one is likely to hear every quarter of an hour, applied indiscriminately.

– Italo Calvino

Two ideas – or more exactly, two obsessions – rule Kafka's work: subordination and the infinite.

– Jorge Luis Borges

I often think of Kafka … He represents something I carry inside me.

– Paul Auster

1

It is precisely 8:07 a.m. when the Boss calls P. into his office. P., who has never met Mr. Hatfield, wonders what he could possibly want. Truth be told, the Boss's secretary was unapologetically straightforward: "The Boss wishes to see you right away." Impossible to guess, from the tone or content of this terse order, whether this was good or bad news. The verb "wish" might lead one to expect a friendly meeting but the adverb "right away" suggested a certain impatience. Some sentences, P. finally tells himself, say nothing more than what they say. So after drawing a line in the bottom-left margin of the document he is verifying for accuracy, P. puts down his pencil, adjusts his tie, wipes the dandruff off his shoulders and promptly makes his way to the Boss's office.

The secretary opens the door and invites P. to go in. Standing at the window with his hands clasped behind his back, like a man contemplating his empire, the Boss stares out. Merely a few seconds elapse between the moments the secretary closes the door and the Boss addresses P. Evidently, the Boss is not a man to waste time – whether his or his employees' – with formalities such as "Pleased to meet you." Without turning around or even acknowledging the presence of his employee in the room, the Boss explains the situation in a few brief sentences and asks P. whether he feels up to the challenge. After P. agrees without a hint of hesitation, the Boss takes out a wooden box, carefully opens it and produces a small envelope. He then turns to P., making eye contact for the first time, and hands him a tiny ticket stub.

What is the nature of the task so casually entrusted to an employee he doesn't know from Adam? Simply this: P. must fetch a hat recently acquired by the Boss at an auction.

"It's a one-of-a-kind," says the Boss, "and I'm giving you this delicate mission because I trust you."

According to Mr. Hatfield, the hat once belonged to a long-dead writer whose novels "marked the adolescence" of the man now at the head of an important New York firm. P. replies that his hat is in good hands and, as if to show his skills in the matter, takes his own hat, carefully puts it on his head, respectfully salutes the Boss and goes in search of the precious headgear.

Outside, P. hails a cab. After exchanging a few banalities with the driver about the weather, chronic traffic jams and the New York tourist season, P. settles in the back seat and watches people and buildings go by. He has been working for Stuff & Things Co. only for a few weeks, so this "mission" is a surprising vote of confidence from an employer who, apparently, never talks to new employees. Hired less than a month ago, P. not only had a private meeting with the Boss, but the Boss even confided in him! He talked about literature! And his adolescence!

P. thinks about the gossips who, day after day, talk behind the Boss's back. "People are so jealous!" he muses. Unlike the stories circulating during morning coffee breaks, the Boss seemed perfectly correct – a true gentleman. P. suddenly feels ashamed to have taken part in earlier backstabbing sessions. He takes a deep breath as if to erase embarrassing memories from his mind, crosses his legs and looks straight in front of him.

When P. sees the huge port cranes, he leaves his guilty thoughts behind. To his great dismay, he realizes he can't remember the name of the author. He only remembers it's a short name that starts with the letter *K* and ends in *a*. Strangely, in the moment, the name reminded him of a Lebanese or Greek dish. So starting with the only dish that comes to mind, he tries to redo the process of identification in reverse. He takes out his notebook (the same notebook he should have pulled from his pocket when the Boss said the name of that poor writer who died bare-headed!) and starts writing variations of "spanakopita": Kapsakapita, Kasnanopika, Kanospikata, Kaskonapita, Kapkasapita, Kassipapikata. Those names seem too long.

P. decides to cross out the middle syllable. The list becomes: Kapita, Kaska, Kanta, Kasta, Kapta and

Kasta. Then he notes two things: first, none of the names reminds him of the writer with the hat; second, Kasta appears twice. P. declares this statistic of two worthy of hope and writes the word "Kasta" at the top of a new page. That way, the names that, from a basic mathematical point of view, have little chance of leading to the desired patronymic won't clutter his mind. P. hates when useless ideas clutter his mind. Raised in the purest Protestant tradition, in a small town in the American Midwest, he sees chaos as the mother of all vices, specious arguments and fallacious conclusions. There is only one way to arrive at the truth: by removing, one by one, in a methodical way, all the falsities strewn in the path leading to Reason.

While P. is thinking about possible variations of "Kasta," the cab reaches its destination. P. pays the driver, climbs out of the car and walks towards a building. From the sidewalk, not only is it impossible to determine the number of storeys of the grey and monolithic tower, but P. cannot make out the different floors. The vertical line is completely uninterrupted and the skyscraper gives a strange impression, similar to what one may experience watching a starry sky or contemplating a log fire. For a fraction of a second, P. feels minuscule in front of this pyramid-like monument erected to the glory of the State Administration.

There is something about the concrete and finite structure that is indefinable, impalpable, even contradictory. As if it were limited and unlimited at the same time, finite and infinite. P. shakes off the feeling and goes into the lobby. Once inside, he notices a large board and concludes it is the building directory. He pulls from his pocket the ticket stub the Boss gave him and finds, without any difficulty, the appropriate Customs Office Department: suite 1934.

The number reminds him of the year 1934. As he walks towards the elevators, he wonders what was significant that year. Hitler's appointment as Reich Chancellor in 1933 and the end of Mao's Long March in 1935 immediately come to mind. But in 1934, nothing.

"Something must have happened," he mumbles.

Four elevators wait in the centre of the building. Since there are forty floors, two elevators stop at every floor up to the twentieth floor, and two go straight to the twentieth floor and stop at every floor after that. Our man cannot believe his luck. Since he is going up to the nineteenth floor, he can choose either option. He can go directly to the twentieth floor and walk down one floor, or he can risk stopping a maximum of seventeen times before he reaches his destination. Although the doors of a "1 to 20" elevator are the first to open, P. decides to wait for an "express" that will take him directly to the twentieth floor.

P. cannot resist the temptation to follow, on the display above the closed doors, the progression of the elevator he let go. When he sees it stop briefly on the twelfth floor and, after pausing for a few seconds on the eighteenth floor, start to head back down, an almost imperceptible sigh escapes him. "If I had taken that elevator, I would be there by now," he tells himself. Meanwhile, the "express" elevators, which are making many a stop between the fortieth and the twentieth floors, don't seem inclined to head back to the ground floor. The fourth elevator, immobilized on the third floor, hasn't moved.

In the end, the elevator that P. let get away is the first one to come back. Is there a way to calculate the probability of the same elevator being the fastest twice in a row? P. ponders that question while the elevators go from floor to floor, following a logic he cannot begin to guess. Obviously, the "human" factor makes the whole thing more difficult to understand. Human nature being for the most part unpredictable, and elevators being for the most part used by humans, it is practically impossible to predict elevator behaviour. For P., this is not only an irrefutable syllogism but it is the quintessential axiom of sound management. His years managing, coordinating, mentoring and supervising people have provided him with countless opportunities to validate this hypothesis. But since the elevator doors are about to close, he cuts his reflection short and, without taking the time to evaluate the pros and cons of his action, jumps in and presses 19.

Later that day, when P. will have a chance to think back on the series of events that led him, within the space of a few hours, from the comfort of his New York office to the crowded highways of New England, he will point to this first irrational – or, at the very least, "precipitated" – act. He will tell himself, as he watches the trees along the road and starts dozing off, "If I had thought about it before jumping in that elevator, I wouldn't be here right now." But let's not anticipate: P. presses 19.

On the third floor – that same floor where the fourth

elevator seems to be stuck – his elevator stops. Assuming employees are going to get in, P. moves to the side and stares at his feet. A few seconds later, he is still staring at his feet – the elevator doors did not open. He waits a bit longer. He clears his throat twice. After waiting longer still, he pushes the button that should open the doors. Nothing. He looks at the button and reads out loud, “Open.” He presses it a second time. Still nothing.

P. wonders, “What is this button for if it doesn’t open the doors?” He approaches the elevator control panel and considers the other possibilities. Other than the most obvious option, which is to bang on the doors and call for help, he can either press the Emergency button or use the red phone. However, his education, as much as his experience in the workplace, has taught him to favour dialogue and to opt for purely mechanical solutions only as a last resort.

So choosing the negotiation option, P. picks up the phone. He waits several long minutes before a nasal voice comes on. The person identifies herself, but so fast that P. cannot make out what she says. Actually, he does make out something, but clearly the woman did not say, “The gator’s waddle and Syrian lumber, geez.” So he says, “Hello?”

“Yes?”

“Good morning, ma’am. I’m stuck in an elevator.”

“The elevator’s model and serial number, please.”

“I beg your pardon?”

“The elevator’s model and serial number, please.”

“I don’t know what they are, ma’am.”

“Without those numbers, I can’t open a file.”

"Okay. Where can I find the numbers?"
"I have no idea, sir."
"You have no idea?"
"I have no idea, sir."
"You can't expect everyone who uses your elevators to find the serial number without any help whatsoever!"
"They're not 'our' elevators, sir. They don't belong to us; we're only responsible for their maintenance. If you have any questions about our company, I'm happy to transfer you to the Vice-President's office. They'll be able to explain the nature of –"
"All right, all right, just a minute. Let me open the control panel and see if it's written inside."
P. reaches for the small door, but sees the following warning: Open Only in Case of Emergency. Is this really an emergency? Can he wait longer or choose another course of action? Is this his only recourse? P. takes a step back, as if creating distance between the panel and his person could give him a better perspective on the situation. After hesitating a few seconds, he reaches for the small door again and tries to open it. It resists. Surprised, he pulls harder. Nothing. He leans forward to take a closer look. He notices a tiny lock to the left of the handle. He picks up the phone.
"Yes, ma'am?"
"Yes?"
"I can't open the door."
"The elevator's model and serial number, please."
"That's what I'm telling you. I can't get to them because the panel is locked."
"If you don't have those numbers, I can't do

anything for you. Thank you for calling Up & Down Elevators, Inc."

"Wait a minute, I'm stuck in one of your elevators! You can't abandon me like this!"

"Without the model and serial number, I can't do anything for you. I don't even know what city you're calling from."

"I'm in New York."

"I'd like to believe you, sir, but how do I know you're not in Chicago or Miami or even Montreal?"

"Why would I lie about that? I'm telling you, I'm trapped in one of your elevators. I'm in New York City, in the Old Port building. I don't see why you need the serial number –"

"And the model."

"– and the model to send an emergency team."

"We don't send emergency teams."

"You don't send emergency teams?"

"No."

"Then what do you do?"

"Personally, I fill out form P-3287-S. When I'm done, I give it to my supervisor, who must approve it no later than six hours after the call. If, in his opinion, the information is incomplete or seems suspicious, he may call the client. Then, once he's satisfied, he communicates with the police. The police determine the degree of urgency of the request and, if necessary, send an emergency team."

"If necessary?"

"If necessary."

P. sighs deeply. In the process, his eyes migrate to

the elevator ceiling, where he sees, written in huge characters, the following information: MODEL: A-4373, SERIAL NUMBER: 3785938496-FD. He grabs the phone, excited.

"Ma'am?"

"The elevator's model and serial number, please."

"It's model A-4373 and the serial number is 3785938496-FD."

"Thank you. How can I help you?"

"Well, as I said earlier, I'm stuck."

"Stuck?"

"Yes, the elevator stopped and I can't make it go up or down."

"Did you try opening the doors?"

"Yes."

"Did they open?"

"Uh, no."

"At what time did the elevator stop?"

"About twenty minutes ago."

"Why did you wait twenty minutes before contacting us?"

"I didn't wait twenty minutes; I tried opening the doors and called almost immediately after. The phone rang for several minutes before you picked up. And we've been talking to each other for at least ten minutes now."

"Is this your first time stuck in an elevator?"

"Yes, I believe so."

"Do you suffer from diabetes?"

"No."

"Do you have high cholesterol?"

"I don't think so."

"Are you claustrophobic, paranoid, hypochondriac?"
"No."
"Do you experience dizziness or feel nauseous when facing unforeseen and potentially dangerous situations?"
"Uh … No, but how many questions are there?"
"Only three more. How old are you?"
"Thirty-three."
"Are you married?"
"No."
"Do you have any children?"
"No."
"Thank you. I'll forward your request to my supervisor. Thank you for calling Up & Down Elevators, Inc., and have a great day."

The lady hangs up and P. finds himself, so to speak, alone again in the elevator. Knowing he will most likely have to wait several minutes, if not hours, before the emergency team frees him, he takes off his hat and his jacket. He neatly folds the jacket, sets it down in a corner of the elevator and sits. He loosens his tie and glances at his watch. This is no doubt an unexpected and upsetting turn of events, but P. can put this time to good use. He closes his eyes and mentally replays his earlier conversation with the Boss. This is a well-known mnemonic device; by re-immersing oneself in a situation and replaying the scene in one's head, one can see and hear things that might have been overlooked the first time. P. tries to piece together everything that was said and done during his meeting with the Boss. But unfortunately for him, he cannot hear Mr. Hatfield say the name of the dead writer who so marked his adolescence that he decided, at 8:07 a.m., to send P. to fetch his hat.

P. takes out his pencil and notebook, and continues the exercise he started in the cab. The idea of a Greek or Lebanese dish previously led him to "Kasta." Now he needs to find a way to go further. He repeats the word out loud several times: "Kasta, Kasta, Kasta." "There was no *s* in that name," he also says out loud.

Although short, the name he is looking for sounded cold and guttural. Probably suggesting the absence of an *s* because that letter tends to soften words. As in, for example, "susurrate," "sigh" or "souvenir." So he replaces the *s* with a more percussive consonant. He proceeds methodically, in alphabetical order: Kabta, Kacta, Kadta, Kaf …

Just as he is considering this fourth possibility, the phone rings. P. leaps from his makeshift seat and picks up the phone before it has time to ring a second time.

"Yes?"

"May I speak with Mr. P.?"

"This is he."

"My name is Sergio Fortunato. I'm the Complaint Department Supervisor at Up & Down Elevators, Inc."

"How are you?"

"Very well, thank you. I have your form here in front of me and, according to your statement, you're stuck in one of the elevators for which we provide maintenance."

"That's right. How much longer do I have to wait before the emergency team –"

"One thing at a time, Mr. P. Your form shows several

incongruities so, if you don't mind, I'd like to ask you a few questions."

"Incongruities?"

"Yes. For instance, I read here that you waited twenty minutes before calling us."

"I think the lady I talked to made a mistake. When she asked, it had indeed been twenty minutes since the elevator had stopped, but she didn't ask until at least ten minutes into the conversation."

"That's what I don't understand. It's the fifth question down, so it's unlikely Ms. Diaz would have waited ten minutes before asking it."

"Well, I had a hard time finding the serial number."

"It's written in large letters on the ceiling."

"I know that now, but I didn't think of looking up at the ceiling when I called. And the lady couldn't help me find the information."

"Ms. Diaz fills out forms. She doesn't know anything about elevators."

"But if you, yourself know that the serial number –"

"And the model."

"– and the model are written on the ceiling, why not tell Ms. Diaz so she can inform the victims –"

"Are you insinuating that Ms. Diaz doesn't do her job well?"

"Not at all. I'm only trying to improve the process. I –"

"You should know that Ms. Diaz has been with the company for more than twenty years and that she would never do anything to unnecessarily prolong the wait of one of our clients."

"I apologize if I came off as offensive ..."

"I accept your apologies and will pass them on to Ms. Diaz as soon as we're done with this conversation. Now, to get back to your file, we were saying that you couldn't find the model and serial number even though, according to our experts, they're visible from more than a hundred yards away. Also –"

"If I may interrupt, whether they're visible from a hundred yards or a hundred miles away makes no difference if you don't know where to look."

"Indeed, Mr. P. That's why we conducted extensive analyses on this very subject."

"Is that so?"

"Of course! According to our experts, in 99.4 percent of cases, a person stuck in an elevator looks up at the ceiling within thirty seconds after the elevator stops."

"And why is that?"

"We don't really care. We manage elevators; we're not psychologists. What's important to us is to predict our clients' reactions in order to offer them the best possible service, not to understand their deep motivations. We can predict this reaction in 99.4 percent of cases. I'm sure you'll agree with me that's more than acceptable in a field where humans are directly involved. So you are, in that respect, what we would call a statistical anomaly. Or, to use a less technical phrase, the exception that confirms the rule."

While Mr. Fortunato explains in great detail the methodology used in the latest studies of elevator malfunction, the margin of error of the latest surveys and the importance of a representative sample of "clients," P. wonders why he didn't react like everyone else. He is, after all, a rational man. He loves playing chess. He reads articles on project management and public administration. Every night before he goes to bed, he takes a few minutes to reflect on his day. He takes his planner and reviews all the steps he wrote the night before. Then he determines what needs following up and plans the next day: he jots down a to-do list in a small notebook and puts it in his jacket pocket. This ritual is to P. what a prayer is to a believer – a moment of daily reflection that allows him to take stock of his life, to evaluate the merit of his past actions and to anticipate future ones. Put another way, this ritual allows him to improve. He performs the task standing up, next to his bed. Once he is done, he slips under the covers and grabs the book on his bedside table (invariably a self-help manual). He then reads for exactly fifteen minutes, switches the light off and falls fast asleep.

But according to this Mr. Fortunato, he is now in the camp of people he loathes – irrational, unthinking, unpredictable people!

"Mr. P.! Are you there?"

"Yes, yes," answers P. "I'm sorry, I'm here."

"The information you provided has allowed us to establish your exact location: you're in one of the elevators of the Old Port building in New York City."

"Yes, I know. That's what I said to Ms. Diez –"

"Diaz!"

"I'm sorry, Diaz, at the beginning of our conversation …"

"Mr. P., do you know that a feeling of profound confusion is one of the first 'normal' reactions of a victim stuck in an elevator?"

"No, I didn't know."

"Well, it is. Not only do we know that now, but we have known that for several decades."

"…"

"Since the Zimmermann case, to be precise. The man got stuck in Miami but claimed he was in Chicago. After every elevator in the city was thoroughly and systematically searched, his body turned up in Florida. He died of a heart attack."

"Well, once again, I apologize but –"

"Of course you apologize! Once we realize we're talking out of our hats, we always apologize! It's a common reaction. Because we tell ourselves, 'I can read and write, I can act like I know everything, like I can apply my massive knowledge to any subject!' I don't know what you do in life, but I assume you don't appreciate getting advice from people who know nothing about your job anymore than I do. In fact, you should know, Mr. P., that people like me, who for years have been helping people like you get out of trouble, have had more than enough of your paternalistic attitude and that …"

While Mr. Fortunato goes on lecturing him, P. hears a familiar sound. He turns around just in time to see the elevator doors open. Grabbing his hat and jacket as quickly as he can, he jumps out. The doors immediately close behind him.

P. looks left and right, then puts his clothes back on. While he is adjusting his tie, the elevator bell rings and the doors open again, as if the elevator were inviting P. to give it a second chance. He could jump in; it is unlikely the same scenario will unfold. Whatever problem caused the elevator to stop for almost half an hour must be resolved by now, thanks to an unflagging team of engineers. Convinced that, statistically, the chances of reliving the same situation are negligible, and aware that he cannot lose sight of his mission, P. heads towards the elevator. At the same time, the bell announcing the second elevator rings. Although he believes in his probability analysis, P. decides to take the second elevator. Just as the doors of the first elevator close, the doors of the second elevator open. It is jam-packed. A very small woman, probably the last person to join the mass of individuals pressed against each other, looks at P. and shrugs – the universal gesture that communicates the idea generally associated with the word "sorry."

P. expects someone to step out, otherwise why would the elevator have stopped? But the doors close again without anyone breaking away from the compact mass of flesh and bones that swelled with each new floor. So P. finds himself alone in front of two elevators with closed doors. He presses the button and waits for about ten minutes. Thanks to the displays above the doors, P. can follow the journey of the two elevators. During those ten minutes, he notes, among other things, that the elevator in which he got stuck goes to the twelfth floor without stopping once; that after this uninterrupted ascension, it stops on the fifteenth, seventeenth and nineteenth floors before coming back to the ground floor. It has not moved since.

As for the second elevator, it seems stuck between the eleventh and twelfth floors. Its occupants are about to face collectively what P. had to face alone. Based on his recent experience, as well as his observation – just as revealing – of the elevators' "behaviour" over the past ten minutes, P. decides that he cannot trust those things. So he opts for the stairs.

There are stairs at either end of the hallway. P. goes to the right. When he reaches the door to the stairs, he reads, written in red letters on a white background, the following command: Use Only in Case of Fire. P. looks at the other end of the hallway. Is it possible that one staircase is used in case of fire and that the other is open to the public? P. goes towards the other staircase. Along the way, he checks his watch. It has now been an hour and seventeen minutes since he left his office. He hurries up.

On the second staircase door, P. reads the following warning: Opening This Door Will Automatically Set Off an Alarm. P. looks back at the other end of the hallway. Why the nuance between the two warnings? The first, urging people to open the door only in case of fire, and the second, stating that opening the door will "automatically" set off an alarm? P. doesn't get how such a distinction can be useful. He understands the function of the first staircase, which should only be used in case of fire. But if there were a fire, wouldn't we want the opening of any door to set off an alarm? If so, why not simply repeat the second warning?

P. considers going back to the elevator. Because, what would the Boss say if he heard that the employee in whom he put his trust caused a commotion, either by unnecessarily setting off the alarm (which would result in the evacuation of the building), or by being arrested in a staircase closed to the public (which would result in either a fine or an embarrassing call to his employer)? P. has no difficulty concluding that neither one of these scenarios is desirable. In both cases, Mr. Hatfield would be justified in thinking that, contrary to what he believed at 8:07 a.m., P. is not the man for the job. In other words, the use of either staircase would betray the trust vested in P., and put an end to a promising career at Stuff & Things Co.

P. goes back to the middle of the hallway and watches the elevators again. He sighs. Then, just as he is about to press the button, resigned, a revolutionary thought crosses his mind: why not knock on one of the office doors and ask for help? This idea – that fulfilling his mission doesn't have to exclude the help of a stranger – makes him smile. He is used to managing by himself but, no matter how resourceful one may be, one cannot do everything alone. He even remembers writing, in one of his precious notebooks, a quote that said something about the need to help each other in the workplace. Although he is outside the strict limits of his workplace, P. concludes that the advice from the self-help guru applies perfectly. He promptly goes to the nearest door, happy about the usefulness of books.

P. knocks on the door. He adjusts his tie and makes sure his jacket is buttoned correctly. He holds his hat in his left hand. He clears his throat once or twice, like a man getting ready to say something important. He waits a few seconds but nothing happens. He knocks again, a little louder this time. He clears his throat again and runs his hand through his hair. After a few seconds, he stares at the doorknob. His entire future is going to unfold behind this door. Someone will tell him how to get out of this maze, he'll find the hat and go back to the office. The Boss will congratulate him. He'll invite him for a drink to celebrate the happy conclusion of P.'s first mission. A friendship will blossom. The Boss will say to P., "Can I call you by your first name?"

"Of course."

"Listen, P., you're doing very good work. But you're capable of so much more. Would you like to become my partner, my associate?" Or even the ultimate vote of confidence in the business world (and a several-hundred-year-old trick to keep wealth and power in the family): "I'd love to introduce you to my only daughter."

P. turns the doorknob. He had no time to picture the inside of the room but has, somewhere in his brain, a general idea of what it should look like. An approximate a priori such as: a smiling receptionist gesturing for him to wait while she answers the phone; then, still smiling, asking how she may help. This classic idea, this archetype of what is behind any respectable office door, was formed during P.'s years looking for work and solidified when he became an employee of Stuff & Things Co. All doors having more or less opened on this more or less identical tableau of a more or less smiling receptionist, it is logical to infer that the current door won't depart from the rule. But an entirely different reality awaits him.

The door is unlocked. He pushes it and slowly walks in, as if visiting an old friend in the hospital he would be careful not to wake. He looks around. He feels slightly dizzy. The room is gigantic. For a moment, P. has the distinct impression that this warehouse is bigger than the building that contains it. About thirty feet from the door, behind a minuscule table where an old man in uniform sits, rows of shelves rise several feet high.

It looks like the private library of a giant. P. cannot make out the boundaries – neither the ceiling nor the walls – because they disappear into the darkness. Only the security guard's table is well lit. He approaches it and sees that the old man in uniform is sleeping. From this new vantage point, P. can now make out the contents of the shelves: suitcases. Hundreds, no, thousands of suitcases. Of every colour, shape and texture. Where are they from? Who do they belong to? And, most importantly, what can they possibly contain? P. clears his throat and says, "Excuse me!"

The security guard doesn't move.

"Excuse me, sir!"

Nothing. A little louder this time, "Excuse me, sir. I'm looking for the Hat Room."

P. has no way of knowing whether there is such a thing as a "Hat Room," but after seeing this room filled with suitcases, he postulates that the building must be subdivided into thematic rooms: suitcases, hats and – why not? – frock coats and umbrellas. That is how the brain of a rational man works: from the somewhat partial observation of a reality until then unknown, it can induce the organization of the whole.

The old man's arms are crossed and he seems to be reading a newspaper – the classic position of a security guard sleeping on the job. P. scans the room and approaches the man. He doesn't like touching strangers, but he has no other choice than to extend his arm and touch the sleeping man's shoulder with the tips of his fingers. The light pressure exerted by P.'s fingers is enough to upset the fragile equilibrium that allowed the man to sleep while pretending to read the paper. The man falls sideways as if P. had hit him with all his might. P. backs up and looks around. Although the chair didn't move, the man has remained in a seated position and is now lying on the ground as if seated sideways, his arms still crossed. P. kneels next to the body. He puts the same two fingers on the old man's throat and feels for a pulse.

For a few seconds, nothing moves in the huge Suitcase Room except P.'s fingers. They walk softly on the old man's throat, searching for a sign of life: two fingers walking the line between life and death; two fingers trying to establish communication between the heart of one man and the brain of the other. Once it becomes clear that the man is dead, P. drops to the floor. Leaning on his hands and knees, he closes his eyes and frowns. He stays like that for several minutes, a single question bouncing in his head: "What should I do?"

Action leads to knowledge, which leads to action, which leads to knowledge, which leads to action, and so on. P. came to this building to accomplish a very specific task, but what he learned is now forcing him to do something different. This never-ending tango between action and knowledge – referred to as the art of dialectics – is both the strength and flaw of the human race, as well as what distinguishes it from animals. Indeed, let's imagine the same scenario in the middle of the Amazon rainforest, far away from civilization. An animal arrives in a clearing and finds a body. It sniffs it out and discovers it is dead. What does it do? If it belongs to the vulture family, it sits down for dinner. Otherwise, it goes on its way. It doesn't wonder, "Should I reanimate it? Should I bury it? Should I search its pockets in order to establish its identity and contact its family?" Finally, and most importantly, it doesn't think, "Should I hide the body so my mission won't be jeopardized?"

P. decides that he needs to hide the body. And where does one hide a body in a room full of suitcases? The answer is so evident that P. sighs: in a suitcase, of course ...

Before hiding the security guard's body, P. decides to draw a work plan. He takes out his notebook and writes, in capital letters: "OPERATION CADAVER." He then writes the numerals one through ten in the left margin. P. knows from experience that not all work plans include ten steps. But seeing these markers on the page helps structure his thoughts and creates a logical sequence between the different steps. "Step 1. Make sure no one is watching." After writing this sentence, P. reasons that someone could be listening but not necessarily watching. So he replaces "watching" with "spying on me." Satisfied with this first step, he moves on to the second.

Should he first find a place to hide the body or should he move the body as quickly as possible, not knowing exactly where he will hide it? P. sides in favour of the second option; it's better to move the body as quickly as possible. So he notes: "Step 2. Hide the body." But he realizes this action raises an important strategic question that needs to be thought through. If he doesn't act right away, someone might come in and see the security guard's body by the table. Conversely, if he moves the body but finds no place for it, someone might see him "with" the old man's body. Anyone catching him with a dead body on his shoulder would be tempted to conclude, rather accurately, that P. is trying to hide it. Which would be terribly incriminating.

However, if someone were to show up while the body is lying on the floor and P. is walking around, looking for a hiding place, he could pretend to be looking for help. So P. concludes that, for now, it is best to leave the body where it is. He even adds, *in petto*, "If I hear footsteps I can always hide."

P. crosses out numeral two and, immediately to its left, writes the numeral three. On the next line, he writes the numeral two and connects it to numeral three with a curved double arrow. Under "Step 2," he writes: "Find a place to hide the body." He then rereads the three steps in order and concludes that they form a logical sequence. But as he is about to write "Step 4," he notices how the first three steps highlight the urgency of the situation. "It might be better to implement the first three steps before thinking about what comes next," he thinks to himself. So he notes: "Step 4. Implement the first three steps right away." He closes his notebook and turns to the giant bookshelves towering behind the unfortunate man.

As it turns out, they are not bookshelves but rudimentary storage shelves like the ones found in warehouse stores or store warehouses. As mentioned earlier, the first row faces visitors. Or: it is parallel to the dead security guard's desk. Needless to say, the shelves don't extend from wall to wall, otherwise it would be impossible to navigate. A space a few feet wide, located dead centre, makes it possible to access the back rows. Since there is no ladder – stationary or portable – P. figures that to put a suitcase on the top shelf, one has to resort to a forklift. Since he has never operated this kind of vehicle, and doesn't hold a licence authorizing him to do so, he will have to hide the body at ground level.

P. has no clue how the shelves have been organized. The most commonly used sorting method in materials management is alphabetical order, followed closely by chronological order. There are, of course, other ways of organizing information. One can use what is called a qualitative value scale, where objects are positioned according to their importance, value or uniqueness. In the field of international trade – a field P. knows particularly well – shelves can be divided into regions of the world, countries or cities.

In the present case, since P. doesn't know the contents of the suitcases and the reason for storing them, he cannot guess what logic determined their organization. For a fraction of a second, he considers searching the security guard's belongings. They might reveal information that would help him better understand the purpose of the room. His years working in the archival industry would then allow him to determine what classification system might have best suited the needs of the firm. As he makes his way towards the desk, P. checks his watch, then stops. Compelled by a strong need to take action, to move forward, he resigns himself to proceed without having all the necessary data at his disposition. Then, because every man needs to justify his choices, he mumbles, "Anyway, I don't really need this information."

Indeed, does P. need to understand the purpose of this warehouse in order to hide a body in a suitcase? What would he gain from discovering that it is simply a place where lost luggage is stored? Had he listened to his professional instinct and searched the dead man's drawers, he might have found information that would have prompted more questions. Those questions, in turn, would have led to more actions that, no doubt, would have brought up even more questions … "Basically, by wanting to know everything, we end up completely paralyzed," P. concludes philosophically. According to this logic, and contrary to what we are taught from our earliest childhood, knowledge leads to inaction. P. turns around, but cannot resist pursuing the argument: had he discovered that this was a storage room for lost luggage, would he then have wanted to know whether the suitcases were from domestic or international flights? Were they abandoned in train stations or …

A noise suddenly interrupts P. and makes him swing around. Someone is knocking at the door. Without having to consult his notebook, P. knows he has only two options: to hide or to open the door. In an act that could be described as the perfect synthesis between theory and practice, he opts for the first option while simultaneously throwing himself behind the closest row of shelves. Lying on his stomach, holding his breath and sweating profusely, he listens to what is happening on the other side of the door a few feet from his hiding place. Remembering having once read that people who lose a sense manage to increase the efficiency of the others, P. closes his eyes hoping he will hear better. He then tries to validate this hypothesis by closing and opening his eyes every ten seconds. He notices no improvement in his hearing. He figures there may not be anything to hear. Or perhaps such auditory compensation is not automatic. Just as he closes his eyes for the third time, he hears knocking again. This time, it is much clearer! "The technique seems to work," thinks P., before remembering that he too knocked a little louder the second time.

The knocking stops. P. waits a few minutes and opens his eyes. He stands up. Partly out of curiosity and partly out of instinct, he pulls apart two suitcases and looks at the door through the slit. Because the floor is black, he immediately spots a white envelope near the door. Now, he cannot presume that the knocker slipped the envelope under the door. Someone else could have done it while he was busy looking for the man's pulse or writing notes in his notebook. P. pushes the suitcases back in place. He takes out his notebook. Contrary to what he established when he wrote the first three steps, P. considers that the first step should be to secure the room. The intruder didn't come in but could have because, as evidenced by P.'s presence, the door is unlocked.

P. estimates the distance between him and the door to be around thirty feet, or ten metres. He opens his notebook and calculates how long it will take him to run to the door. He remembers running a hundred metres in fourteen seconds when he was in college. He adds one second to account for his age, one second for his lack of training and two seconds for his business clothes and dress shoes. He looks at his notes and, to be on the safe side, adds another second. Assuming a speed of a hundred metres in nineteen seconds, he should reach the door in less than two seconds. If someone were to knock just as he takes off, he would get there before the intruder turned the doorknob or knocked a second time. He would then block the door with his foot and, catching his breath, lock it in a flash.

P. tiptoes to the end of the row. He sets his goal, inhales deeply and shakes his hands along his body (something he does without thinking, probably a remnant of his track-and-field days). He springs forward. Before he has taken three steps, a sharp pain seizes his calf. He does all he can to avoid screaming, but the pain is so intense that a yelp escapes his tightened lips. Acting of their own will, his hands fly to the rescue of the calf in distress. This sudden, even instinctive movement takes the rest of P.'s body by surprise and knocks it off balance. As he crashes to the floor, P. hits his elbow hard causing him to scream a second time. Between the moments he felt the pain in his leg and found himself curled up on the floor, less than two seconds have passed.

P. lies on the ground a dozen feet from his objective. His right hand pulls his left leg towards him while his left hand clutches his right elbow. His lips are clasped and he is breathing through his nose. Just as he opens his eyes, he hears someone knock on the door.

Clearly, P. is in a precarious position. Though his years studying information management have taught him to handle every situation like a project to be managed, taking into account resource availability; though he knows that every project has its share of unpredictability; though he has learned to make do with all kinds of unfortunate setbacks; though he knows, in a word, that one should not abandon but rethink one's plan in order to accommodate new data, P. finds himself "hoping" that the intruder will leave without insisting.

Of course, P. knows that this hope has no scientific or rational basis. The chances of the intruder actually behaving in this way are real. That's undeniable. But they're not real "because" the first intruder behaved in a similar way. P. tries to reason with himself: "Being in a precarious situation is no reason for giving up." After all, he can't just stay there and do nothing. If someone opens the door, he or she will see a dead man sitting sideways next to his chair, and another man writhing in agony a few feet away from him. What would that person think? That the two men got into a fight and the one who survived killed the other. Or, he or she might think the two men were attacked by a third who took off with a bunch of suitcases. This scenario reassures P. enough to try to stand up.

At the same moment, the door creeps open. P. freezes and decides to pretend he is dead too: he shuts his eyes. He hears someone shuffle in. He also hears a sort of creaking he cannot identify; maybe the man (or the woman, why not?) is pushing a cart piled with suitcases.

P. hears the door close behind the visitor. Then more footsteps and creaking. Plastic rattling. Or perhaps a small marble rolling on the floor. Finally, he hears a voice.

"Is someone here?"

P. opens his eyes. How can he go unnoticed? He's curled up smack in the middle of a gigantic empty space! P. has to turn around to see the man coming towards him.

"Is someone here?" repeats the man.

P. turns his head to the right and, over his shoulder, sees a small man dressed in black, walking with a white cane. He wears dark glasses. It is clear that he is blind.

P. can hardly believe it. Seconds ago, he thought he was done for. The door was going to open, and he was going to be charged with the murder of a security guard. Or worse, the Boss was going to call the Customs Office to ask where his employee was. He would be told that yes, his employee came by earlier but was now in jail.

"In jail!" the Boss would say.

"Yes, he was charged with the murder of an old man."

"Murder! An old man!" the Boss would exclaim.

Of course, the man may not have been assassinated. He may not have been the victim of a killer but simply of a heart attack. However, P. knows that appearances speak louder than words and that, once charged with murder, no matter the outcome at trial, his career will be over. The Boss will explain that he is happy to hear P. is not a vile assassin, but it makes no difference: he has failed his mission and the Boss can no longer trust him.

"Roger, are you here?" asks the blind man.

"No, he had to step out," answers P., surprised to hear his own voice.

"Oh, okay. Can you tell him that there was a fire in the Hat Room?"

"The Hat Room!" exclaims P., painfully propping himself up.

"Yes, nothing serious, but they have to send some hats to the dry cleaner."

"To the dry cleaner!" repeats P.

"Yes, but not all the hats. The ones in row 'A to M' escaped the smoke. They asked me to tell you they're going to bring the hats here while they clean the room. It shouldn't take more than three or four hours. Is that okay?"

"Yes, I'll make sure to tell Roger."

"Where did he go?" asks the blind man.

P. kicks himself for saying the name of the security guard. Had he simply said "thank you," the blind man would not have inquired about Roger. But on hearing his name, he was reminded that the person he came to see was not there. The situation is all the more serious that it now forces P. to lie.

"He said he had something to take care of. He should be back in …"

"In … ?"

"In twenty minutes," P. finally says.

"Oh. Well, I won't wait for him but I'm counting on you to tell him what's happening. Goodbye now."

"Goodbye."

During the conversation, P. inched his way towards Roger's desk. By the time the blind man says goodbye, he is standing in front of the old man's body, as if to hide it – as if the blindness of the intruder had not been established convincingly enough. After the dead man's colleague shuts the door behind him, P. hops to it and locks it. He then leans his forehead against the door and shuts his eyes. Not like a man seeking sleep but like a man needing to make an important decision quickly. In less than two seconds, this decision becomes clear: if, as he believes, the hats are organized in alphabetical order, and his hat actually starts with the letter *K*, it should be in the "A to M" row that will soon be brought to the Suitcase Room. There is no time to waste.

P. slides onto the floor and, leaning against the door, grabs his notebook. As a reminder, the first four steps previously written by P. were: "1. Make sure no one is spying on me. 2. Find a place to hide the body. 3. Hide the body. 4. Implement the first three steps right away." The intruder's episode messed up the sequence, but every good employee must know how to deal with unexpected events. Those don't diminish the importance of P.'s plan; P. simply needs to modify the plan to fit the new reality.

In locking the door, P. effectively addressed the first step. So he can put a check mark to the left of number one. This action brings him great pleasure or, to be more precise, it gives him the satisfaction of a job well done. Indeed, nothing is more satisfying to P. than to check off the steps written in his notebook. Right now, his rate of completion is 25 percent. Although it's not bad, it's also not enough. But P. can make it better. He understands the importance of professional motivation, so he's going to use a proven method to increase his average! He's going to add additional steps that correspond to actions he has already taken. Below "Step 4," he writes: "Get rid of the intruder." And on the next line: "Lock the door." P. cracks a smile. After the steps have been freshly recopied and renumbered, he can check off three out of a total of six. A 50 percent average! Emboldened by this result, he moves on to the next step: "Find a place to hide the body."

P. goes to the suitcases. On the way, he glances at Roger: "Thank God he's small." In the first row, he notices trunks and some of those big duffle bags athletes and outdoor enthusiasts like to use. He approaches a large blue trunk, grabs the handle and, as best he can, drags it off the shelf and into the centre aisle. For a reason P. cannot explain, a mirror hangs on the inside of the shelf. P. briefly glances at it, then leans over the trunk. He notices with relief that the lock was pried open. "What a job," he muses, thinking about the poor guy who, day after day, must pry the locks off abandoned suitcases and inspect their contents.

P. lifts the lid. The trunk is overflowing with old newspapers. They are, for the most part, classifieds from the *New York Times*. He digs a little and finds a sports section and more classifieds. P. figures the owner must have used newspapers to protect the trunk's contents. He digs deeper and discovers an impressing quantity of books.

After rummaging through the yellowed paper a bit, he pulls out *Mond über Manhattan* by a certain Paul Auster. P., who doesn't read German or know Paul Auster, leafs through it anyway, as if he were in a bookstore, looking for a book to take on vacation. After a few seconds, he puts it down and digs in the trunk again. He cracks a smile; this activity is rather pleasant. Like being at an amusement park or about to open a treasure chest. The second book, also in German, is titled *Das Sandbuch* and was written by a certain Jorge Luis Borges. Like a kid allowed three presents, he digs in the trunk a third time, all the way to the bottom. Still in German: *Herr Palomar* by Italo Calvino. P. then sees, between two classified sections, something he had not noticed: not a German book, but a thick yellow envelope. He opens it and finds an untitled manuscript – an anthology of short stories. The first story is titled "Reading on the Bus."

As we alluded to earlier, P. is a serious reader. He reads books on management, self-help manuals and, less frequently, biographies of men who have amassed huge fortunes or put faltering businesses back on the path of profitability through sheer determination and will. Of course, he read a few novels when he was in college, but he has never bought a book of fiction simply for the pleasure of reading. Yet, though time is short because he has a body to hide and a hat to find, and without knowing exactly what is motivating him, P. closes the trunk, perches himself on top of it and, like a man sitting on a park bench, starts to read – an action, however concrete and real, that is nonetheless fundamentally irrational. The mirror makes the scene even more unreal because it looks as if P.'s twin brother is reading the same book.

Reading on the Bus

The man is standing on the sidewalk of Anna Blume Boulevard, reading. He is holding his book high in front of his face, a somewhat ridiculous position for anyone used to the comfort of a favourite armchair, a cozy bed or a good old straight-backed chair. The effect is all the more disturbing because the man in question wears a hat. From a distance, his head seems shaped like a book covered with a hat.

A careless observer might think he is hiding behind the book, like in those detective novels where spies peer through two holes punched in a newspaper. But one with a keen sense of observation will immediately understand the meaning of this scene. This man, who reads standing up, is waiting for a bus. He knows from experience that if he focuses exclusively on the book, he will miss his bus. He also knows that if he constantly lifts his head to see whether the bus is coming, he won't understand what he is reading and will have to reread the same page a dozen times. So he found a way of reading comfortably by adopting a position that maximizes his peripheral vision.

Our reader doesn't face the direction of the oncoming buses. He has developed a far superior technique: he finds a passenger who regularly takes the same bus as him, and parks himself with his book immediately to the passenger's right. Then, as soon as he detects a movement from the corner of his eye, he lowers his book and climbs on board. As long as the person doesn't decide to go visit their mother or move to a new neighbourhood that day, the technique is infallible.

All of a sudden, the man lowers his book, confirms with a quick glance the destination of the bus stopping in front of him and climbs on board. The bus is packed. Pressed together like sardines, men, women and kids fight for a piece of territory according to a set of unspoken rules. The sit-downers hang on to their catch while the stand-uppers surreptitiously follow the sit-downers' every move. The war between the two clans knows no respite. When one of the sit-downers gets up, the mass of stand-uppers becomes agitated by a common goal until the coveted seat is occupied again. A collective sigh follows as everyone re-examines the human checkerboard and plans his or her next move.

Holding his book under his arm, our man looks left and right. He gets up on his tiptoes and tries to see, in the back of the bus, if an empty seat might have escaped the other passengers. Nothing. Resigned, he slips the book in his briefcase and grabs one of the straps dangling lazily over his head. He stands for at least fifteen minutes before the seat immediately to his right becomes available. He slumps into it and, before he even has time to settle in, reaches for his briefcase and takes out the book.

This seat is far from ideal. Because it faces the bus's central alley and one must sit sideways instead of facing forward, every time the bus turns or brakes, one gets tossed every which way. Passengers must constantly fight centrifugal force. In addition, the comings and goings of people climbing on and off is a constant source of frustration for anyone trying to read. But in any case, our man now opens his book.

He is reading a well-known American author's most recent novel. The main character – a man in his thirties – rides buses from dawn to dusk. He is a writer by profession and has decided, for his latest novel, to sit in the same place a well-known black woman sat years earlier, refusing to give her seat to a white man. He retraces that journey over and over again, and observes the dynamics between blacks and whites. This key incident in the fight against segregation is now part of the American psyche, part of the collective imagination. Insofar as the author can intelligently integrate this "common literary space" – as he calls it – into a modern narrative, it will most likely earn him a Pulitzer Prize.

Meanwhile on the bus, still grappling with centrifugal force, our man looks up, hoping to find a more suitable place for reading. Since no seat has been vacated, he goes back to his book. He is presently reading a reflection by the main character. The latter finds it unfortunate to live in an era when other people's gaze, and the judgment that accompanies it, has come to dictate our every move – as if our ability to think was located outside our own bodies, as if our individual consciousness was nothing more than the sum of other people's perceptions of us. And, the character notes with emphasis, "We always fall prey to the dictates of appearance."

As the man reads those lines, something strange happens. He thinks about modern man's proclivity to act according to the gaze of others, and wonders whether this analysis applies to him. Because he has stopped reading, he is now able to look up and he sees that a seat in the back of the bus is becoming available. Between the moments he sees the person stand up and, a fraction of a second later, decides to stand up too, several things happen: first, an old black woman sits immediately to his right; second, his brain makes a connection between this woman and the old American woman in the novel; third, he doesn't want anyone to "think" he is racist because he stood up at the exact moment the woman took her seat; and, fourth, he sits back down pretending to move his hat to prevent the woman from sitting on it.

The story, if we can call it that, ends there. P. closes the manuscript. He has no idea what to make of it. If he had to summarize it for a friend, he would simply say, "It's the story of a man who's reading." Nothing happens in this story. In fact, it is not even a story because reading a work of fiction, as depicted in the manuscript, is not active. It is passive. Having studied a few classics in school, P. remembers that he was asked to talk not just about characters but most of all about action.

P. goes to the security guard's table and puts the manuscript next to his hat. He goes back to the trunk and starts emptying it. Since the body will take up the entire trunk, he realizes he also has to hide the books. He cannot leave them on the floor – that would tip off any passersby. He takes a look around and rapidly concludes that the best solution is to slip one or two books in each of the suitcases in the first row. So for about ten minutes, P. goes from the trunk to the suitcases and, like a fair-minded Santa Claus, slips one or several books in each suitcase depending on how much space is available.

Once the trunk is empty, P. looks at the old man's body and wonders whether he should drag the trunk to the body or the body to the trunk. Choosing the second option (more practical, because it doesn't involve dealing with the weight of the trunk and the weight of the body), P. goes back to the body. The man weighs little, so P. has no trouble carrying him to the trunk. As he lifts the body to drop it in the trunk, he notices its rigidity; he cannot move the security guard's limbs. Frozen in a seated position, the body might not fit in the trunk. P. sets it in anyway, and though the man's head and shoulders stick out, he tries to close the lid. "Only three more inches," he tells himself. Without putting all his weight on the lid, because he doesn't know what consequence this would have, P. struggles to accomplish his task. Impossible. The man is so stiff, unless P. breaks his legs or his neck, he cannot possibly close the lid.

P. steps back to get a better look at the trunk. The head is still sticking out. He thinks about the story he just read. About that man who reads standing up, with the book directly in front of his face. A man with a book for a head and a trunk full of books with a head! Going back to his task, he decides that the sitting position is only one of several possibilities. Like those kids' games where one has to rotate a shape to figure out how to insert it in the appropriate opening, P. grabs the old man's feet and pulls them towards him. Roger falls on his back. Again, P. takes a step back. Now the feet and lower legs are sticking out. He rotates Roger by a third of a turn. This time, the dead man's behind is sticking out unattractively. Having, so to speak, examined the question from all sides, P. concludes that the body is too big for the trunk. Or the trunk too small for the body.

Determined to keep on course and not alter his plan, P. searches for another trunk. He goes from row to row, until he finds a blue, white and red bag that looks like it could do the job. He drags it next to the trunk as best he can and opens it. It is filled with hockey equipment and exudes a rather unpleasant stench of sweat. P. takes Roger out of the trunk, transfers the contents of the hockey bag to the trunk and stuffs Roger in the stinky bag. He then closes the bag without any difficulty and, after putting it back where he found it, rubs his hands with a satisfied look on his face.

After getting rid of the security guard's body, P. unlocks the door so the man bringing the hats will be able to come in. Then he goes to the small desk where the poor guard laid his head for the last time, puts a hand on the metal chair and, after some hesitation, sits down. He takes out his notebook and adds another step to his list: "Wait for the hat delivery." P. then rests his elbows on the green desk blotter and his chin in his hands.

One could mistakenly think that P. is stupidly staring at the door. But though we have not had the chance to describe P. in detail – to paint a picture of his personality and, through a proven technique that consists of telling the story of his childhood, to understand the man he is today – a keen reader will have guessed that P. is a serious man. Indeed, doesn't our first impression of P. come from this image of a man who draws a line in the bottom-left margin of the document he is verifying for accuracy, puts down his pencil, adjusts his tie, brushes the dandruff off his shoulders and promptly makes his way to the Boss's office? Everything is there.

Even if we described P.'s office which, by the way, consists of two chairs, a work table, a grey file cabinet and a wooden coat hanger; even if we added that no artwork, no photograph and no plant brings a personal touch to this work environment; and even if, postulating an inevitable relationship between an individual's work environment and his deep self, we added that other than the three pens, green desk blotter, small calendar and black phone, nothing clutters said work table, well, that would not change in any way the impression created by that first image of a man putting down his pencil, adjusting his tie ... and all the rest. Precise action, more than a description of place, defines to the letter the man you know, fittingly, only by the letter *P*.

So P. is sitting at Roger's table. He takes a deep breath and crosses his arms adopting, without realizing it, the position in which he found Roger. Exhaustion doesn't arise solely from physical effort. Situations of great stress can also drive the body to regenerate. Through sleep, of course. And so P. dozes off in the exact spot where, a few minutes earlier, he discovered a man who had closed his eyes for the last time. As we know, that man has become, through a strange set of circumstances, exactly what he was in charge of protecting before his death: the contents of a bag. Like an undertaker, who after a lifetime preparing bodies for burial becomes a body that must be buried, the security guard has become an object that must be guarded.

The reader won't be surprised to learn that P. soon starts to dream. We are not in a position to accompany him on the adventure his brain concocts for him, but we can easily imagine the presence of "classic" symbols. It would be perfectly reasonable to assume, for example, that P. will dream he is falling. The surroundings and the location of the fall are of no importance. Whether P. falls from the Eiffel Tower or the Grand Canyon matters little to the story. The fall, as a symbol of chronic lack of affection or fear of the future, is more important than the context. In the present case, we can safely say that P.'s uncertain future is the source of his anxiety.

Maybe P. dreams he is in a suitcase thrown out of a plane that will never reach its destination. We can imagine him, his head sticking out of the suitcase, screaming at the top of his lungs while plunging into a bottomless abyss. Because the brain has the ability to integrate countless little details from recent experiences into our dreams, it is possible that P. is screaming in German or, even more likely, that a hat is falling at the same speed as the suitcase without ever crossing its trajectory, sentencing P., like a modern Tantalus, to see the object of his quest until the end of times without ever being able to reach it. But all of this is pure speculation. What we know is that the dream is short-lived and ends abruptly, because P. wakes with a start minutes after closing his eyes.

Presently, P. is thinking. He is thinking that, in a few minutes, the hats stored in row "A to M" will arrive. He will only have to find his (yes, he has appropriated it), make sure it is in good condition and leave this damn building. Of course, and as always, this raises an inevitable administrative question. If P. simply takes the hat without showing the stub the Boss gave him, he will more or less have "stolen" the hat. It is not hard to imagine what will happen next: a thrilled Boss will thank P. by throwing his arms around him. He will offer him a cigar and a glass of that delicious cognac he saves for special occasions. Then a few days later, a furious Boss will call P. into his office and shove a letter under his nose. The letter will say that, due to a fire, some hats had to be moved and, regrettably, the Boss's hat can no longer be found.

The Boss will demand explanations. He will fire off a series of questions, not so much to get answers but to demonstrate P.'s unforgivable lack of judgment in the affair. Of course, one of the questions will be the following: is the hat that is prominently displayed behind him, and that fills him with pride, actually Kabta's (or Kacta's, Kadta's, etc.) hat, or is it just any hat P. found at a discount store? P. will have to admit to either his incompetence (he was incapable of following the procedure required to fetch the hat), or his crime (he ignored a several-hundred-year-old administrative rule that stipulates whoever takes possession of a hat must first sign a register).

P. takes out his notebook and writes, in capital letters: "SCENARIOS: 1. Go back to the office and explain everything to the Boss (consequence: the Boss will accuse me of being incompetent and fire me right away). 2. Wait for the hat to arrive, take it and hurry back to the office (consequence: in about a week, the Boss will accuse me of being incompetent, he'll call the police and I'll end up behind bars). 3. Wait for the hat to arrive, take it and –"

A siren cuts short the elaboration of the third scenario. A large door P. had not noticed before creaks open and a small forklift – like the ones used to move objects too heavy for common mortals: wood, bricks, metal, hats – appears. The vehicle approaches P. at a tortoise pace and, stopping a few inches from the desk, lowers a huge crate to the floor. A few seconds later, the driver waves to P. and disappears, closing the door behind him.

P. looks at the crate. To his surprise, the planks are not nailed in; the lid is simply resting on top of the crate. P. has no trouble removing it. He sees sixteen hats. He grabs the closest one – a shapeless, old, brown aviator helmet, with black fur trim obviously meant to protect the pilot's face from the cold. P. flips the hat over to look at it more closely and notices a white piece of paper tied to it with a string. He reads the tag: Howard Hughes (1905–1976). He sets the hat aside and grabs another one – a gangster fedora from the forties. He puts it on his head but, having forgotten about the mirror on the inside of the shelf, cannot judge the effect. He puts the hat back in the crate. He digs around for several more minutes before finally putting his hand on the hat that, in theory, belongs to the Boss – a small and well-worn black hat *à la* Charlie Chaplin. The tag says Franz Kafka (1883–1924). That's it: Kafka. P. now remembers the name.

P. pulls out the hat. He flips it over and over in his hands as if it were a strange object he was seeing for the first time and couldn't guess its function. He wonders what could have motivated a man like the Boss – a man who can buy anything he wants – to spend money on such a thing. Aesthetically speaking, the hat has no value. Any respectable circus has a multitude of similar hats in its collection. So, clearly, the Boss didn't acquire it for its looks. Nor did he buy it with the intention of wearing it. No one buys a hat without trying it on first! Especially not the Boss – a proud man who shops in New York's most elegant department stores. This hat, P. muses, must "represent" something. It must not be an object but the representation of an idea or value that is dear to the Boss. Knowing nothing about Kafka's work, P. cannot speculate what values it might have transmitted to the hat, assuming that books can transmit values to hats.

He puts the hat on his head and an idea bursts forth. Even though he has not yet fully written Scenario 3, he knows what he's going to do. He knows his life is about to take a turn, that he's not the person he thought he was. The man who only cared for columns of numbers and documents filed in the right place – as stipulated by best practices and procedures – was a lie. Worse, that man was a slave whose ability to think in a rational manner had been co-opted and put in service to people he didn't even know. P. knows the era of information management is over. He will strike out on his own! No more bosses asking him to go fetch hats!

Now that he has performed his last filing by stuffing the security guard in a hockey bag – owned by a certain Paul Doucet from Montreal, Quebec – P. is working up the nerve to do something radical for the first time in his life: he's going to steal a hat. He can't even imagine how the idea crossed his mind. Through what neurological process did the matter that makes up his brain conclude he must not only steal a hat, but that he must steal the hat the Boss asked him to fetch? And once this decision was made, how was he able to take it one step further and say in a low voice, "Not only am I going to steal this damn hat, I'm going to ask for a ransom"?

The reader, for whom this story is not a first foray into the world of crime and delinquency, will understand that this is a fairly common phenomenon. Small crimes lead to more serious crimes. Crime doesn't follow the logic of arts and crafts, where satisfaction comes from small benefits and the repetitive nature of an activity is pleasurable in and of itself. Crime follows the logic of savage capitalism: it must grow or perish. How else could we explain those stories about billionaires who steal millions before getting caught red-handed?

And so P. juggles with the idea of a banal crime – stealing a hat – to then move on, within seconds, to the idea of a major crime – extortion. We will see, in the following pages, whether P. will turn out to be a pragmatic criminal able to contain, or even stifle, the expansionist logic of the profession he is about to embrace, or whether he will fall prey to the muses of large-scale crime and, God forbid, go so far as to murder the Boss.

P. takes a step back, gauges the height of the crate and guesses it must contain four rows of sixteen hats. In other words, sixty-four hats! He first considers asking the Boss for a ten-thousand-dollar ransom. Of course, this number is arbitrary, because he has no idea how much the Boss paid for the hat, or how much celebrity hats are worth on the black market. That said, P. calculates that if he were to take all the hats, he could live worry-free for many years.

While he is weighing both sides of this new scheme, a practical question interrupts his train of thought: how would he obtain the list of the different hat owners? Or worse, how would he carry all those hats? He doesn't own a car or truck. And he can't exactly call a moving company! No, all things considered, it's better to stick with his first idea and limit himself to the Boss's hat even if it means asking for a twenty- or even thirty-thousand-dollar ransom.

"It's a shame that I don't know Kafka," he thinks to himself. "I'd be in a better position to determine the amount of the ransom. Was he a great writer? What did he write? Action-adventure novels? Historical novels? Strange stories like the story of the reader reading in a bus? Why does the Boss care so much about his hat? Did Kafka write about his family in one of his novels? Or is Kafka himself part of the Boss's family? The names Hatfield and Kafka have nothing in common but plenty of immigrants changed their names when they came to America!"

The idea of a potential family connection between Kafka and Mr. Hatfield comforts P., because it opens up the possibility of an objective link between the hat and the Boss.

In addition, this idea touches him. So for that reason, and also because he is fundamentally honest and every honest man perpetually wages war against his own contradictions, he reconsiders for a few seconds his decision to kidnap the hat. "All I have to do is get out of here, explain everything to the Boss with a good laugh and I'll be all set. If criminal charges are pressed, the Boss, for whom the hat is the most important thing, will stand up for me. He'll defend my integrity and won't stop at anything to make sure I come out of this ridiculous adventure with my reputation clean. He'll go so far as to offer me a promotion for having made the success of the mission my one and only consideration. He'll say to the media waiting to hear him publicly explain the Kafka hat affair, 'This kind of situation is not unusual in our overly bureaucratized world.'"

"Overly bureaucratized world"? P. is stunned. Did he really formulate that thought? Did he really say, in his heart of hearts, the words "our world"? Did he really take a sarcastic position "against" the world? While he was imagining what the Boss "might" think and say, a dormant thought deep inside him was awakened. An opinion he didn't know he possessed surfaced out of nowhere and entered the imaginary mouth of the Boss. Of course, P. has opinions. He's human. But as far as he knows, he has always been in favour of the world. He has always defended the established order, the usual way of doing things. He has always advocated that due respect be paid to experience and, when innovation knocked on his door, he opened it very cautiously.

P., a sociologist might add, is fundamentally conservative. He wants to preserve the world in which he lives. But although he still hesitates between the optimistic path of goodwill and the more troubling path of crime, this "critical" thought foreshadows the end of any re-examination of the criminal path. To put it another way: although P. has always maintained that experience reinforces the established order, he notes that his own experience caused a fundamental change in him.

Before his troubles with unpredictable elevators and security guards dying on the job, P. never found bureaucracy problematic. For him, it was synonymous with division of labour, rational organization of the workload and, by extension, increased efficiency in project management. Period. He has no patience for those who attack the heavy infrastructures of his firm. To see bureaucratization as the curse of "our world" is therefore a blow to his conception of the world. Like a man holding on to a dream rendered impossible by its contact with reality, P. sighs, grabs Kafka's hat, his own hat and the manuscript, and makes his way to the door with slow and weary steps.

In the hallway, P. is confronted with another sad reality: the reality of the elevators. For the first time since childhood, something strange happens inside him. As he looks at the button he must press to leave this floor and start his new life, an almost forgotten feeling arises. It begins with what we call, probably for lack of a better word, butterflies. They invade the lower part of his abdomen and, like monarchs migrating north once a year, start to twirl around his heart, which reacts to this sudden attack by beating a little faster and, it seems to him, a little "stronger." Then something even stranger happens: the elevator doors become blurry and dance in front of his eyes. Within seconds, what was perfectly clear dissolves into a blurred and fluid image. P. is crying.

The elevator doors open. The elevator is like a cursed cave one must travel through in order to one day see the sun again. P. enters like a condemned man resigned to leave the world of men. His slumped shoulders recall the shoulders of men forever banished from their ancestral village. His drooping head is not unlike the heads of women on their way to the stakes of the Inquisition. When the elevator doors close behind him, P. sighs like those men who have lost everything or those women who don't recognize anyone anymore. This mechanical contraption, ruled by scientific principles, should not provoke such feelings. We live in a mechanized world. Every day, we use devices whose workings we don't completely understand, yet that doesn't stop us from trusting them. But trust between P. and this mechanized world – this world created by men to address the needs of men – has been broken. And this break has an even more tragic repercussion: it has broken the link that tied P. to the world of men.

When P. entered the elevator earlier today, he belonged to the world. An entire social network explained his presence in this building: parents who met at school, got married in a church and had a son, born in the hospital of a small town in the American Midwest; a more or less normal education; a year spent in Chicago, where he lived with his uncle and worked odd jobs; and finally, a New York employer who gave him a mission to fetch the hat of a long-dead writer.

His entire life seems to have led him here, to this elevator. And what about the future that would have awaited him had he accomplished this unusual task? The ultimate reward for his success would have been felt for decades. In the short term, P. expected, of course, an increase in salary and, who knows, maybe a little performance bonus. But more importantly, he expected recognition from the Boss and his colleagues for a job well done. He firmly believed the Kafka hat anecdote would have become the cornerstone of a brilliant career and, in the long term, would have allowed him to climb the corporate ladder. He would have alluded to it not only at high-society events, but also at international conferences where, as an invited guest, he would have spoken about the vicissitudes of success and failure, and the importance of discipline and a job well done. But this glorious future was not meant to be.

Just as P. is about to press the button and turn his back on a life of honest work, he hears someone scream, "Wait!"

P. instinctively stops his movement towards the control panel, and redirects his hand towards the doors, which he holds out of courtesy for the stranger now getting in.

"Thank you," says the young woman with a smile.

"Uh … What floor?" asks P., staring at the panel.

"Ground floor, please," answers the woman.

P. presses the ground-floor button and takes a few steps back. He is holding Kafka's hat in his left hand and the manuscript under his arm. His right hand, however, is at a loss. He slips it in his pants pocket, but takes it out right away, thinking that it makes him look too casual. He then puts it in his jacket pocket but, before the elevator reaches the ground floor, he removes his hand, imagining the aristocratic air that this position must exude. Out of pockets and ideas, he finally lets his hand hang "naturally" by his side. To P.'s great displeasure, the elevator is not going down but up.

"You're afraid of the cold?" asks the woman.

"Excuse me?"

"I see you have two hats, but only one head," she says, indicating Kafka's hat with her chin.

"Uh, yes. I mean no, I'm not afraid of the cold. It's another hat. I mean this hat belongs to me, of course, but … actually, I just bought it."

"I see," says the woman.

With a quick head turn to the left, P. looks at the woman from the corner of his eye. In less than a second, he is able to "capture" her image and can now observe her mentally without having to look directly at her. She is blonde. Her long hair flows softly over her shoulders and takes on gold and copper hues. The hair is, as they say, silky. No doubt, it would feel soft to the touch. P. even ventures to think it must smell good. It is the most beautiful thing he has seen in a long time.

P. coughs nervously. He is about to add something about the origin of the hat in his left hand when the elevator stops.

The woman bursts into laughter and says, "Again!" Before P. has a chance to do anything, she starts banging on the doors and screaming, "Help! We're stuck in the elevator!" P. is filled with wonder. This woman took less than a second to assess the situation. Or, in less than a second, she assessed it and sprang into action. P. steps back and takes in this strange spectacle of a woman banging on the doors with both hands and screaming for help … with a smile on her lips!

"Come and help me," she says with this smile that never seems to leave her.

P. steps forward and starts banging with one hand.

The woman looks at him, amused, grabs Kafka's hat, puts it on her head and says to P., "You'll be more effective like this!" After a moment of hesitation, P. throws the manuscript on the floor and continues banging, now with both hands. Then, without knowing why, he bursts out laughing. It begins with a smile but, in less than five seconds, he is laughing out loud and banging on the doors as if his life depended on it.

Had he been alone in the elevator, P. would have probably closed his eyes for a few seconds in order to assess the situation. He would have recalled Mr. Fortunato's words and Ms. Diaz's questions. Then he would have looked up, like 99.4 percent of people stuck in an elevator, to make sure the elevator model was still written on the ceiling. Next, he would have picked up the phone and given the information to Ms. Diaz. He would have waited for Mr. Fortunato's call and, no doubt, would have been less aggressive with the Up & Down Elevators, Inc. employee. But this procedure, although more rational than the one he is now fiercely implementing, won't be necessary.

P. is about to scream, "Help!" but the woman suddenly stops banging and brings her finger to her lips. P. freezes. The woman listens and, to P.'s surprise, the two prisoners hear a voice tell them they know they are there and are coming to get them.

"The emergency team should get us out of here soon," says the woman, out of breath.

She is still wearing Kafka's hat. P. takes a few steps back. He adjusts his tie. The woman asks, "Is this the first time this has happened to you?"

P. answers without thinking, “Yes.”

He has no idea why he just lied about something so banal. He reasons that his criminal instinct must be taking over and that, from the moment one chooses a life of crime, one has to fully assume it. Up to this moment, he has never had to “protect” or hide parts of his life. But things are different now. His adventure in the elevator marks the first chapter of his new life and, as such, he must keep it secret. Indeed, had he not gotten stuck on this particular floor, he would not have knocked on the door of the Suitcase Room. Had he not found, then hidden, the security guard’s body, he would not have been there when the crate full of hats arrived. Had he not decided that his only viable option was to steal the hat and, to avoid setting off the alarm, to take the elevator again, he would not be here with this pretty woman wearing the incriminating evidence on her head.

While waiting for the emergency team, P. wonders how to get his hat back. It has been a few minutes now since the voice told them the emergency team was on its way. The woman has sat down in a corner of the elevator and taken a book out of her purse. Looking P. straight in the eye, she says, “Does it bother you if I read while we wait?”

“Not at all,” answers P.

So she is now engrossed in her book, Kafka’s hat still on her head. To accommodate her reading position, from time to time she adjusts the hat, as if she had owned it forever. If he says to her, “Can I please have my hat back?” she might think there is something special about it and start asking questions. So P. decides to wait for a more opportune moment. That said, he knows that when the emergency team shows up, things may unfold quickly and the pretty woman could take off with Kafka's hat. That would be the worst-case scenario. If P. loses the fruit of his crime, he will not only prove that he is a thief, but that he is an incompetent thief. He doesn't even dare dwell on the consequences of such an outcome.

The woman suddenly bursts out laughing. Standing by the elevator's control panel, like a bellboy from the old days who would ask, "What floor?" P. looks at her and smiles politely.

"You must read this story. It's only a few pages," she says as she hands him the book.

It doesn't even occur to P. to flip the book over to see the author's name or title. For the second time in less than an hour, he simply starts to read – this time, a short story titled "Borges and Mathematics."

"Huh, Borges," says P.

"You know him!"

P. knows better than to reveal how he discovered Borges – while emptying a trunk full of books in which he was trying to hide a dead body. He simply says, "Not very well," and starts reading.

Borges and Mathematics

In his book *On the Edge of the Book,* Cliff Thornston takes on Borges's labyrinthine imagination. At the end of a fifteen-year study of Jorge Luis Borges's work, the famous American mathematician claims that, with the help of software he designed himself, he managed to boil the Argentinian writer's entire literary creation down to a single mathematical figure.

This eccentric American, who admits not having read "so much as a single short story" by Borges, says he wanted to prove that literature and mathematics use the same logic and that the two disciplines are trying to prove the same thing: the finite nature of the universe. Two disciplines that use the same logic and are trying to prove the same thing are, in Thornston's eyes, one and the same. Consequently, literature doesn't exist except as a subcategory of mathematics. In an article published in the *New York Times* that explains his approach, Thornston writes:

I have always found literature's universalist pretentions ridiculous. But I am a man of science, so it is without any negative a priori that I began the study of Borges's work. Personally, I have nothing to prove; I simply want to move science forward. My conclusions, and the equations I used to get there, speak for themselves. Those who might want to attack these conclusions will have to demonstrate that I made a calculation mistake. To that end, I have included, in the book's appendix, all my formulae and described all my experiments with the precision and objectivity that scientific rigour and intellectual honesty demand.

Thornston explains that, as a first step, he replaced every letter in Borges's prose with a corresponding number ($a = 1$, $b = 2$, $c = 3$, etc.). The word "Borges" thus became 2.15.18.7.5.19. Then, once Borges's entire body of work was translated into digits, Thornston turned his attention to punctuation. He admits thinking for a few years that this puzzle might defeat his entire enterprise. There was something arbitrary and non-scientific in the attribution of those functions. In an interview with the BBC in 1987, he went so far as to admit that "whether punctuation has intrinsic value may be more a matter of philosophy than mathematics, in the sense that it is not about the meaning given to clauses but about the relationship that unites, divides or separates those clauses."

Thornston spent four years on punctuation before discovering what he calls "the principle of functional rotativity." Indeed, Thornston discovered that, no matter what function he attributed to the different punctuation signs (comma = addition; period and capital letter at the beginning of a sentence = opening and closing of parentheses; semi-colon = subtraction; etc.), after 111 rotations of these functions, there was a stabilizing effect, meaning that there was no point in attributing this or that function to this or that punctuation sign. After 111 rotations, the answer to the paragraph was "stable."

With this victory, he felt a surge of confidence and started looking into paragraphs and chapters. He quickly came to the conclusion that there was no fundamental difference among paragraphs, chapters and stories. Knowledge being necessarily cumulative, it was logical that data from a chapter or paragraph would "build" on top of data from the rest of the work. On this subject, Thornston writes: "Whether data from an equation, a formula or a hypothesis corroborate or invalidate data from what was previously held as knowledge changes nothing. Science is, by nature, cumulative and 'accumulates' these different pieces of knowledge, even when they are contradictory."

Having conquered the theory, Thornston dedicated himself body and soul to proving it. He notes that in the first year, every time he tried to synthesize all the data from Borges's different works, the computer crashed. One of his fiercest opponents, poet James Urquendt, noted with irony that the Borgesian prose, so used to being free, was refusing "to be put into a box by a vulgar machine." Thornston replied in an op-ed to the magazine *British Science* that "the very idea of prose being free is nonsense only a medieval mind can formulate. Letters, words and numerals, with all due respect to Mr. Urquendt, are symbols that refer to either concepts or facts. And neither facts nor concepts can get used to anything. Only humans have this capacity."

Thanks to increasingly stronger computers and sophisticated software, Thornston finally concluded his experiment. On reading *On the Edge of the Book*, we get the impression that the process – not to say the quest – was more rewarding than the result. Indeed, after all those years of experimentation, often plagued with doubts and long waits, Thornston said that once the answer was validated, he felt "some unease." I let him conclude:

> *When my assistant confirmed that the answer had been the same for two weeks, I told myself that the experiment was conclusive and that the mathematical figure was, scientifically*

speaking, correct. However, I didn't expect the figure, written on a piece of paper by my assistant, to provoke such unease. In truth, I didn't know what to make of that number. I knew it "represented" the sum total of Borges's works, yet a part of me wanted to go further and "interpret" that number. To this day, I have stopped myself from doing so because it would be going beyond what science can say about reality. In any case – it bears repeating – since the experiment still hasn't been disproved, I have to conclude that Borges's work boils down to this: 1934.

Nineteen thirty-four? His hand shaking, P. gives the book back to the woman and merely says: "You read a lot?"

"It's my job," answers the woman.

"It's your job to read?"

"Yes. And to write, of course."

"Ah, you're a writer."

"Yes. Actually, I'll be a writer in a few months."

"You're going to publish your first book?" says P.

"Exactly."

"Congratulations!"

"Thank you," says the woman, touching Kafka's hat with the tips of her fingers the way a cowboy would salute.

"What is it about, if you don't mind my asking?"

"It's about a man who, for years, has been trying to publish a book about his three favourite authors. Then one day –"

"Who are they?" asks P.

"Three great writers. In my opinion, the greatest writers of the twentieth century: Jorge Luis Borges, Italo Calvino and Franz Kafka ..."

"Franz Kafka!" exclaims P.

"Yes, the Czech novelist. You don't like him?" says the woman, straightening up her hat.

"Uh, I don't know him that well," says P. "I know he died a long time ago. I know he used to wear funny hats," he jokes in order to change the subject.

"Oh yeah, I love that picture with the hat. You're referring to the picture of young Kafka with his dog, right?"

"Yes, the one with the dog," P. instinctively answers, learning by the same token that Kafka had a dog.

"In fact," she adds, "the hat he's wearing in that picture looks a lot like the hat for your second head."

She takes off Kafka's hat and examines it. P. can hardly breathe. It has been less than five minutes since he stole a hat and opted for a life of crime and, just like that, this woman, this perfect stranger, is about to uncover the truth. P. cannot believe it. Out of all the elevators in all the office towers of all the cities in America, why did she have to pick this one? P. takes off his hat and frantically scratches his scalp, as if the woman's last comment had caused a violent and uncontrollable allergic reaction.

The woman, who is examining the hat from every angle, shows it to P. and says: "It's incredible; don't you think it looks like it?"

P. is about to collapse.

"Uh, yes, it does, although it seems a bit small."

The woman looks at the hat again, then puts it back on her head.

"You're right. Unlike what people think, Kafka was kind of tall. Although you can be tall and have a small head," she adds with a smile.

"That's what I think too," says P., putting his own hat back on his head.

"But it's still incredible," adds the woman.

"Yes, pretty incredible," repeats P.

P. is suddenly convinced that the woman knows everything. She works for a security agency. The Suitcase Room was fitted with surveillance cameras and she saw everything from her office somewhere in the building. She saw him enter the room, take the security guard's pulse and hide the body in a hockey bag. She watched him pretend he was working for the Customs Agency. She saw him steal the hat and leave the room. Maybe she even engineered the elevator malfunction to make him spill the beans. P. would not be surprised if every single one of his words was being recorded.

"But hey, life is full of coincidences, isn't it?" adds the woman.

The phone rings just as a strange silence falls between P. and the woman. Since P. is already standing, he picks up.

"Hello?"

"Good morning. My name is Sergio Fortunato and I'm calling on behalf of Up & Down Elevators, Inc."

"Uh, good morning," says P.

"May I ask with whom I'm speaking?" says Mr. Fortunato.

"Uh …"

"Is everything okay, sir?"

"Uh, yes," says P.

P. remembers his earlier conversation with Ms. Diaz and decides to play the disoriented victim.

"Listen," says P., "I don't feel so well. But there's someone here who can talk to you."

"Perfect. In the meantime, I suggest you sit down and relax. If you're wearing a hat, take it off. You should also take off your jacket and loosen your tie. Untie your shoes if necessary. The emergency team should be there soon."

"You're going to send an emergency team?" says P. despite himself.

"Yes, of course, but as I said, have a seat and pass the phone to your companion."

"Okay," says P. and, turning to the woman, "It's for you."

The woman looks at him, amused, and grabs the phone. P. steps back and flops down on the floor. The woman's presence allowed him, if only for a few minutes, to forget his predicament but, with Fortunato on the line, reality is fast catching up. Seconds after grabbing the phone, the woman looks up at the ceiling and reads, in a clear voice, the elevator's serial number. She has taken off the hat to better speak on the phone and is twirling the hat around her finger like a toy. P. is dying to grab it from her hands but, as long as they are stuck in the elevator, he knows that would be useless.

"Yes, a man in his thirties," the woman tells Fortunato. "He seemed fine until the phone rang."

P. figures that Fortunato asked her to describe the

other victim. The woman turns to P. and repeats, one by one, the same questions he had to answer earlier.

"Do you suffer from diabetes?"

"No."

"Do you have high cholesterol?"

"I don't think so."

"Are you claustrophobic, paranoid, hypochondriac?"

"No."

"Are you prone to dizziness or feel nauseous when facing unforeseen and potentially dangerous situations?"

P. is about to say no, as he did earlier, but instead changes his answer.

"Yes, I sometimes get dizzy."

"How old are you?"

Once again, P. changes his answer in order to "cover his tracks."

"Thirty-two."

"Are you married?"

"No."

"Do you have children?"

"No."

Sergio Fortunato then asks the woman the same questions. Like P., she is not claustrophobic, paranoid or hypochondriac. She is twenty-seven and unmarried. P. didn't catch her name.

A long silence follows, punctuated by the occasional "okay," "yes," "no," "all right," "I see," "I don't think so." Then P. notices something strange. Mr. Fortunato "called back" even though the occupants of the elevator did not call the company. Yet the procedure described by Ms. Diaz was crystal clear: if, according to the supervisor, the information compiled by Ms. Diaz is incomplete or seems suspect, he may call the client. But no one in the elevator called Ms. Diaz. In addition, Mr. Fortunato is now filling out the form, which is supposedly Ms. Diaz's "unique task."

P. wonders what Fortunato is telling the woman. Are they planning his arrest? Is Fortunato explaining how to draw a confession out of P.? One of the "yesses" he heard might have been in response to a question like "Did you get the hat back?" Panic-stricken and feeling the urge to act quickly, P. takes out his notebook.

He turns to the page on which he started the elaboration of Operation Cadaver. With a shaky hand, he writes on a blank page: "Escape Scenarios." Farther down, he writes the numeral one. He looks at it for a few seconds, then circles it. After a few more seconds, he draws a dash immediately next to it. He retraces the circle two or three times but nothing comes. P. has no idea where to start. Like a writer facing the blank page, who would try to shake himself out of it by writing, "I'm currently facing a blank page and I'm trying to shake myself out of it by writing that I'm facing a blank page," P. writes: "How can I get out of the elevator?"

P. remembers his unease when he first looked at the building from the sidewalk. He had a funny feeling, maybe even a premonition, before he stepped inside. Something in him wanted to say, "Don't go in! If you go in, you'll have to give up any hope of a career. You won't come out unscathed." Something in him. But what? What is this something that's not his brain but that communicates with his brain unbeknownst to him? Does he possess another organ whose existence he is unaware of? An organ that can help with decision making? Or, better yet, an organ whose main function is the preservation of the individual? It must be some kind of instinct. A sort of animal intelligence, however intangible, that informs an individual's choices when his survival is at stake.

"Are you okay?" says the woman as she hangs up the phone.

"Yes, thank you," says P. "I felt a little dizzy."

"Maybe you should take off your jacket; it's getting hot in here."

P. realizes that he is sweating profusely. He notices the feeling of heat in his armpits and feels sweat beading on his forehead and running along his nose. He pulls out a handkerchief and, slightly embarrassed, quickly wipes his face like a kid who has been reprimanded by his mother for a milk moustache. Then he takes off his jacket and undoes his tie, which he slips into his pocket.

"You should also take off your hat," says the woman as she herself puts Kafka's hat back on her head.

P. takes off his hat. A hat, unlike Kafka's hat, that is worth nothing, because P. has never written anything. A hat that is nothing more than felt and glue, because its owner never inspired anyone with his prose. P. bought it last spring after he lost the one his mother gave him when he left home. That hat – P.'s first hat, now lost – was with P. for years. It accompanied him in his job hunt. It saw dozens of films. It walked up and down the streets of New York in search of something to do between work and bedtime. Who knows, had he not lost that hat, maybe he would not be stuck in the elevator today.

P.'s second hat, which he puts down on the floor next to the manuscript, is nothing in comparison. Not the type of man to shop for "the" hat, P. spent very little time looking for it. This hat – his own hat, a hat only worth the forty dollars he paid for it a year ago – suddenly takes on new value. As if it were responsible for P.'s misfortunes. Can a hat change one's life?

P. looks at the woman. She has gone back to her book. What did that writer do to make people fight over his hat after his death? Why is this old hat so important? Why do billionaires, who have better things to do, go in search of hats? He has heard of billionaires collecting cars, houses or even airplanes. But hats? Does the Boss have a hat "collection" or is Kafka's hat the only one he wants to own? Why do so many people want this hat so badly that it prompted its owner to sell it at auction?

The woman turns a page and changes her reading position allowing P. to see the title of her book: *On the Masters' Path: Kafka, Calvino and Borges – Short Stories*. She's reading short stories by Kafka! A sigh of satisfaction escapes P. The woman looks up and asks, "Is everything okay?"

"Yes, I suddenly feel much better."

"I'm happy to hear it."

"I see you're reading Kafka."

"Yes, an anthology of short stories by Kafka, Calvino and Borges. Are you a fan?"

"No, not really, but now I understand why you thought my hat looked like Kafka's hat."

"You're right. Unconsciously, I must have made a connection between the story I just read, Kafka's photo and your funny little hat."

The woman takes Kafka's hat in her left hand. She looks at it with a smile and adds, "You have to admit, the resemblance is stunning."

P. smiles and holds out his hand to take the hat back. He is about to grab it when the elevator doors fly open and a fireman screams, "Quick! Get out of there!"

The two prisoners jump out and, a second later, the elevator falls. The firemen grab them just as the elevator hits the ground with a deafening sound.

Before P. has time to realize what is happening, a fireman drags him towards the stairs at the other end of the hallway.

"Quick," says the fireman, pulling P. by the sleeve.

"What's happening?"

"There's no time to talk. We need to get out of the building."

As the fireman utters these words, he pushes with one hand the staircase door where earlier P. had read: Opening This Door Will Automatically Set Off an Alarm. P. steps into the stairwell and instinctively covers his ear with his free hand to protect himself from the piercing sound that will occur any second. After two floors, the alarm still has not gone off.

"There's no alarm?" he asks the fireman between floors.

"No."

"What about the warning?"

"Warnings are there to limit the use of the stairs. It's psychological."

P. could have opened the door and taken the stairs without setting off the alarm! He came up with ridiculous scenarios and opted for the elevator based on a false premise! P. rushes down the stairs on autopilot. At each landing, numbers written in large red characters on the white concrete wall track their progress. When they go from the fourteenth to the twelfth floor, P. remarks, "There's no thirteenth floor?"

"Of course not!"

"Why not?"

"It's bad luck."

2

Max has been looking at the river for about ten minutes. It is not yet 6:00 a.m. and the fog, thinner than usual, floats above the glacial waters of the St. Lawrence. Standing a few feet from the road, he pulls his hat down to shield himself from the wind coming off the river. He smokes a cigarette, his left hand in his pocket. The blinkers of his car, abandoned on the side of the road, beat like a mechanical heart in the half-light of dawn.

He is frowning so intently, he looks as if he were searching for something. But he is not. He thinks about the river. He comes this way every day, but has never stopped to look at the river before. He tells himself that it is stupid. Tourists from all over spend huge amounts of money to come here and go whale-watching while he, who lives practically around the corner, never bothers to glance at it. Max likes irony, so, as he finishes the cigarette he usually smokes in the car, he smiles from the corner of his mouth.

He wonders whether the same is true elsewhere in the world. Do people who live close to extraordinary sites (the Egyptian pyramids, the Great Wall of China, the Leaning Tower of Pisa, magnificent beaches or mountains ...) ignore those wonders the same way he has been ignoring his river for fifty-five years? He thinks for a few seconds and realizes that this is nonsense. A site that is part of a man's day-to-day reality – a familiar site – no matter how magnificent, is by definition ordinary. What would be extraordinary for someone in Pisa, for example, would be to wake up one morning and see *his* tower gone. The river is simply part of his reality.

This thought comforts him, because he doesn't like the idea of being abnormal. Different, yes. Abnormal, no. He has his habits, his routine, his preferences and believes wholeheartedly that a certain humanistic logic guides his choices. In college, he studied more than just public administration and accounting. He read the "classics," particularly philosophy and literature. He got involved in student politics. He fought for a better world. Even if he would not go so far as to describe himself as predictable, which would be pejorative, he sees himself as reasonably coherent. There.

That said, the question remains: is it normal to ignore the beauty of one's own reality simply because one is exposed to it on a daily basis? Applied to other spheres of life, this rule about the consequence of everyday life on our perception of reality is unbearable. If repeated contact with a given reality prevents us from perceiving its beauty, is the same true about love or friendship? Can we love only what is far away? Max finds this idea peculiar; for him, it is perfectly reasonable to "discover" something that has been right under one's nose but, for all kinds of reasons, one never fully appreciated.

In London, for example, did an Englishman, who drives along the Thames every day, finally stop to look at it just as Max was realizing that the St. Lawrence is, after all, magnificent? Maybe the man is lighting a cigarette as we speak. Of course, there is the issue of time difference but who cares. He looks at the Thames the same way Max looks at the St. Lawrence. To a certain extent, two men looking at two rivers at the same time are a little bit looking into each other's eyes. Max likes this discovery and pushes further: two men looking at two rivers at the same time are probing infinity. Why not? He watches the water flow and, inspired, pushes further still: two men looking at two rivers at the same time are contemplating God.

No, no, no! Now, it's too much! Max doesn't believe in God, so it is ridiculous for him to posit a hypothesis, however poetic, that he cannot fully assume. He goes back to the "infinity" version. He thinks about it for some time, then discards it. It's basically a beautiful formula that means nothing. Contemplating infinity brings one closer to nothingness than to reality, and nothingness doesn't interest him any more than God. No matter what anyone says, man can only look at man. And even then! So he goes back to his first version. That's it, he feels he is looking into this man's eyes. He even thinks he knows why the man stopped to look at the Thames today when yesterday, he drove right past it.

The man got up earlier than usual. He went down to the kitchen without making a sound. He made his coffee in silence. He ground the beans the night before so as not to wake anyone. Yes, everything was planned. He drank his coffee standing in front of the window. In three little sips, like others make the sign of the cross at night before going to bed. Quickly, and without much conviction. A little ritual meant to mark the passage of night to day, to announce the rising of the sun. When it came time to turn off the coffee maker, he noticed it had an Italian name. He thought about his first trip to Florence and, while trying to remember the name of the Sanremo *pensione* where he lived for a month, he noticed a small orange stain on the top-right corner. He tried to scratch it off with his nail. It would not come off. He rinsed his cup and quietly set it down in the sink. Before leaving the house, he took his hat.

Max is satisfied with this version of events. He knows other versions exist but, for now, he finds this one particularly credible. He stubs out his cigarette on a tree trunk and pockets the butt. He says in a low voice, "He must be on his way now." Because the more he creates this Londoner, the more convinced he is that after looking at the Thames for a few minutes, the man got in a car and left London. He might also have gone to the airport – if he had decided to fly to America, for example. He took only a few belongings – a Michelin Guide, some fruit and an old manuscript, which he slipped inside a yellow envelope the night before. He will drive for several hours and, when evening comes, stop for the night. He might even sleep in the car.

Max checks his watch. It is almost 6:00 a.m. He grabs another cigarette, lights it and inhales deeply, as if he expected the river's salty air to clear both his thoughts and his lungs. But nothing happens. His mind turns to the people the Englishman left behind this morning. He must be married and have kids, otherwise he wouldn't have taken the French exit. The French exit! Indeed, why the silent coffee, the stolen fruit and the manuscript if he were living alone? His wife and kids will wake up in a few minutes and realize he is gone. They will look for him. To no avail.

His wife will figure it out right away and pretend everything is fine so as not to worry the kids. She will make breakfast, holding back her tears – sometimes of rage, sometimes of shame. The children will come back from school later that afternoon. The oldest will ask, "Where's Dad? He was supposed to repair my bike this evening."

She will reply that he went on a business trip to America.

The oldest will say, "Since when does he travel?"

His mother will answer that Dad is meeting a very important person in New York. A man known throughout the world, who will help him with his project.

The oldest will ask, "What's Dad's project?"

His mother will say that it is a secret project.

Max throws his second cigarette in the river. He feels bad for this woman who must lie to her oldest son and who will lie again later to her youngest. Does she deserve to have her life turned upside down because of a stupid manuscript? Because Max knows that everything revolves around this manuscript. He knows it is the reason the Englishman left his family. If he could talk to him, Max would tell him to go back home, that risking everything for a few pages scribbled in sweat and blood is not worth it. He would tell him that life – real life – is right here, right now, and that dreams disguised as manuscripts are nothing but illusions.

But life is complex. It's easy to create characters and take sides, to criticize them or indulge them, to make them victims or heroes. He has not even finished creating this woman, for instance, and has already given her the role of the victim. Because she could just as well be at the centre of her husband's decision and play a completely different role. That's a well-used but effective technique: to make the reader believe that the torturer is the victim and to reverse roles at the end of the story. This woman – mother of two – also has secrets, habits and unavowed dreams. Who knows, maybe she is the one pushing her husband to publish. Maybe he's happy to write from time to time, when the kids are asleep. Maybe it's a way to clear his head. That's all.

What if for years she has been telling him he has real talent and should make writing more than a hobby. He should publish! Maybe she tells him he's wasting his life lining up numbers that mean nothing, and moving sums of money from one column to another. He should create something "concrete." Yes, that's it: she contrasts the necessarily abstract nature of numbers to the concrete nature of words. While numbers only represent concepts (quantity, height, weight, etc.), words represent the things themselves.

That's where Max's reflections have led him when he climbs into the car. He drives slowly and, from time to time, looks at the yellow envelope on the passenger seat. Like a taciturn passenger, the manuscript accompanies him on his mission.

After a few minutes, Max sees a woman on the side of the road. She is hitchhiking. Max is not one to pick up hitchhikers, but this time – perhaps for the first time in his life – he slows down, takes a closer look at the woman and stops. She is wearing a pink dress. She put it on earlier this morning and looked in the mirror for a long time. She found herself neither beautiful nor ugly, even with this pretty dress. She never manages to find herself beautiful. When her mother saw her cross the kitchen in a hurry, she asked whether this dress might be too elegant for the restaurant. Why take the risk to stain it or to rip it, especially since no one will see it under her apron? What was she thinking – wearing her best dress to go wait on truckers and farmers? How could she have such bad judgment? The young woman refused to look at her mother, slammed the door and kept her composure. Once in the car, she burst into tears.

Since the restaurant is only a few miles from her parents' house, she decided to stop for a few seconds to dry her tears. She pulled over and parked the car by the river. She took a deep breath, and got out. She hesitatingly walked to the shore. Once she reached the water, she closed her eyes and let herself be rocked by the lapping of the waves. Only a few more steps and all her problems would be solved. The St. Lawrence would take her somewhere else. To a place where mothers don't comment on your every move, where older brothers don't lure you into the barn by any possible means, and where customers don't make fun of you. The river wouldn't judge her. It would take her and carry her far away, to warmer countries. Countries full of wine and love. She thought about Spain or Italy.

She checked her watch. There was no need to rush, so her mind returned to Italy. If she could leave, that's where she would go. She would rent a house by the sea. There would be a flower garden, a yellow and blue boat and a little black cat she would name Gaspé. She would wear long, white cotton dresses and go to the village once a week. Eventually, she would meet a man. This man would be the exact opposite of the men in her village. He would be a filmmaker, an opera singer or even a novelist, why not? His home would be filled with books. He would write tiny little stories. Fables, tales. Improbable stories where people live in trees, where the will to exist is enough to exist, and where you can live fully even when life has knocked you down. In a word, stories where imagination wouldn't compromise. Or better yet, he would have been working for years on his *magnum opus*.

Every morning, the writer – her love – would get up at the crack of dawn and, like a craftsman impervious to the demands of time, he would sculpt words one by one, with infinite patience. One day, he would let her read his manuscript. She would be his first reader. She would live on love, stories about love, fish and red wine. She checks her watch. She suddenly remembers that fish and red wine don't mix. This bursts her bubble, because she doesn't drink white wine. And, come to think of it, she's not crazy about fish either; she prefers cool days to warm days; and men and mothers are probably the same everywhere. "The hell with Italy," she shouts angrily.

She checked her watch again and went back to the car. She turned the ignition. Nothing. Except a small click. She sighed, "Not again!" She knew from experience that there was no use trying again. Her mechanic had told her many times that there was nothing more he could do for that poor car. But the woman cannot afford a new one so once a month she has to walk. Except today, she is wearing a dress and shoes unsuitable for a long walk. So she decided to hitchhike.

She waited on the side of the road for a few minutes before a car slowed down and stopped next to her own car.

"Climb in," says Max, as the woman opens the door.

"Good morning. My car broke down. Are you going all the way to the restaurant?"

"The one at the bottom of the hill?"

"Sam's, yes."

"Yes, I was even going to stop there. Come!"

"Thank you," says the woman as she gets into the car. As soon as she touches the seat, she jumps back up. "I'm sorry, I just sat on something."

Max picks up the envelope, but the woman grabs it before he can throw it on the back seat.

"It's okay, I can hold it."

She puts it on her lap and turns towards Max.

"It's your manuscript?"

"I'm sorry?"

"It's a joke. I asked if it was your manuscript."

"Why do you think it's a manuscript?"

"I don't know," the woman answers, visibly uncomfortable.

Strangely needing to explain herself to this perfect stranger, she adds, "When I was waiting, I was daydreaming about a trip to Italy, about a house full of books and a manuscript. When I saw this envelope, I immediately thought, 'A manuscript.' It's ridiculous, I'm sorry."

Max is stunned. She guessed the contents of the yellow envelope in less than two seconds. His secret project! This novel he has been writing and rewriting for years and that only a few editors have read and rejected. No one in his immediate circle knows that he writes. No one knows that for exactly thirteen years not a day has gone by without him thinking about his manuscript. No matter what he is doing, he thinks about the structure, the characters, the ending. He wonders whether it is too long or too short. He rereads it and changes the narrative voice. He puts everything in past tense, then switches back to present. He inverts chapters to create mystery, then puts them back in order to facilitate comprehension. A manuscript he hides in a safe at the office and never brings home for fear it will fall into the hands of his wife or one of his kids.

"Are you from around here?"

"Yes and no," answers the man. "I'm from Montreal but I've been living here for about twenty years. My name is Max."

"Pleased to meet you. I'm Dora."

"Are you from around here?"

"Not only am I from here, I've never been anywhere else," says Dora with a sigh.

"Really!"

"Oh, once or twice when I was young, my father took us to Quebec City. And I've been to Montreal twice to see jazz concerts. But that's all."

"That's unbelievable!" says Max.

"There are other ways to escape, no?"

Dora looks at the yellow envelope.

"I've never seen you at the restaurant."

"True," answers Max. "I don't usually come this way in the morning. My office is about eight miles in the other direction."

"And this morning?"

Max checks his watch. By now, his wife and two sons must be wondering where he is.

"This morning is different. I'm going to the U.S."

"Boston?" says Dora.

"New York," answers Max.

"New York? Lucky you!"

Max looks at Dora. Here is a young woman who has never left her part of the world. She lives only a few miles from the border and works in a restaurant, so she must have met Americans and speak English. But she has never crossed the border.

"You're going to miss the exit," Dora says suddenly.

Max slows down and stops a short distance from the exit. He leans towards Dora and says, "Listen, I don't know you, you don't know me and this may sound a little strange, but I have something to propose to you."

Dora instinctively puts her hand on the door, ready to jump out. Max says, "Do you want to come to New York with me?"

New York! That city is everything her little village is not: a self-contained universe she feels she already knows from reading about it in so many novels and seeing it in so many films. At the restaurant, not a day goes by without someone mentioning the American metropolis. So she has learned about all its tourist attractions: the Statue of Liberty, Staten Island, the Empire State Building, Carnegie Hall and a multitude of highly praised restaurants.

Whether they are truck drivers or tourists, they all come back from New York with a light in their eyes. Dora has never left Quebec, even though the state of New York is only a few miles from her house. She has been living in the province since she was born, on April 14, 1972. And now this stranger is proposing an adventure. She blushes at the idea that he might expect some sexual favour in return. She looks at her dress, slightly relaxes her grip on the door handle and lays her other hand on the yellow envelope.

"I'm an accountant by profession. I have a wife and two sons. This morning, I grabbed my manuscript –"

"So it really is a manuscript?"

"Yes, a manuscript I've been working on for the better part of the past fifteen years. No one's agreed to publish it yet but last week I had an idea."

"Which is?"

"I was reading Paul Auster's latest novel and –"

"Paul Auster!"

"You know him?"

"Of course. I've read all of his books," declares Dora.

"So you've read *The Brooklyn Follies*," says Max.

"Yes, I just finished it."

"Then you must remember the anecdote about Kafka."

"Uh, remind me," says Dora with a frown.

Max recounts how Auster writes that Kafka invents a story for a little girl who has lost her doll. He explains that his own novel revolves around Kafka's hat and the city of New York. Since one of the greatest New York novelists is a fan of Kafka, Max thought he might agree to read his manuscript and, who knows, maybe even write the foreword!

"If Paul Auster agrees to contribute to my novel, no editor will be able to refuse it!"

Dora doesn't know how to respond. On the one hand, she understands the strategy but, on the other, she thinks it is downright crazy to imagine Paul Auster would play that game. Without having to think about it much, she feels the plan is destined to fail. Not wanting to hurt Max with a critical remark, she asks a technical question: "Did you write your novel in English?"

"No, but that's the beauty of it. Paul Auster reads French. He even worked as a translator at the beginning of his career."

"That's unbelievable," replies Dora.

"Who knows, maybe he'll agree to translate it into English," says Max before bursting out laughing.

"You never know," answers Dora, who now wonders whether she is dealing with a madman.

Maybe this man is spinning a crazy story in the hope of luring her to a dingy motel. Maybe he came to the restaurant two weeks ago while she was reading *The Brooklyn Follies* between customers. He would have noticed she was devouring the novel. She would serve her customers in a hurry and run back behind the counter to read a few more paragraphs, holding the book at arm's length in the strangest position. Throughout the years, she tried many times to find a position that would allow her to be attentive to her customers without spoiling her enjoyment of whatever she was reading. After many unsuccessful attempts, she concluded that the most effective technique is to hold the book high up in front of herself so her peripheral vision is not encumbered by anything other than raised hands demanding her attention. This way, she can both focus on her book and remain attentive to her customers.

This technique makes it obvious to everyone that she is reading. Also, for anyone standing directly in front of her, her head, hidden behind the book, is completely invisible. Which gives her a funny look. It would have been easy for Max to sense the young waitress's distress and to understand that, for her, reading was a sort of escape. He may be neither a reader nor a writer but, before leaving the restaurant, he would have noted the title of the book and bought it the next day. But he might not even have read it. He could have opened it randomly and come across the anecdote about Kafka. An anecdote she remembers perfectly well now. To win her trust, he doesn't need to give her an exhaustive summary; he only has to mention the title and some random detail. So he made up this story about a manuscript, a meeting with Paul Auster and a trip to New York. The only thing true in his story is probably the fact that he is married and has two kids.

She looks at the envelope again. All she has to do is open it to expose the dirty scheme. She'll grab the stack of blank paper – it may even be a section from Saturday's newspaper – pull it out with a theatrical gesture and *voila*! He'll have no other choice than to admit it was an ambush. She'll then jump out of the car, walk to the restaurant, put on her apron, and another day of misery will begin.

That is what the most basic common sense dictates to Dora. However, reason and intuition act as counterbalance and prevent the dominance of one way of apprehending the world over the other. When intuition suggests an approach or a way of assessing a situation, reason steps in and demands accountability. The opposite is also true because reason cannot always prevail. In the present case, intuition is acting as a survival instinct – if Dora falls into a trap, her bad judgment, to use her mother's words, could cost her her life. But instead of trusting this survival instinct, which is demanding that she rationalize what she wants, Dora looks into Max's eyes and asks, "Is he waiting for you?"

"Paul Auster?"

"Yes. Does he know you exist?"

"No, but I more or less know where he lives. I know he likes to walk his dog and I have a picture of him."

"So you're going to wander the streets of New York in the hope of bumping into him?" says Dora.

"Not the streets of New York; the streets of a specific neighbourhood in Brooklyn."

Max delivers this answer without much conviction. As if he has no other choice but to believe it. Dora understands that her own distress might not be worse than his. Here is a man who thought he could escape through writing, but the quest for liberation has turned him into a prisoner. The escape has become a jail. He picked up the pen to escape his routine, but the anxiety of the day-to-day grind has transformed into an unhealthy obsession: to publish at any cost. He is aboard a vehicle – writing – whose speed and direction he cannot control. Like a powerless passenger, he simply waits for the inevitable crash that will put an end to his journey.

Max can see Dora is doubtful. The opposite would have been surprising. He knows his story only makes sense insofar as it remains an idea, an imaginary construct. As soon as one tries to demonstrate how it could take shape, it collapses under the weight of common sense. At best, the story of a man who wants to meet Paul Auster, hoping Auster will read a novel about a man on a quest for Kafka's hat, might make a good novel. Difficult to say at this point.

"Listen, Dora, if you stop and think about it, this makes no sense. Thinking that my manuscript will be published because of a chance encounter with one of the greatest American novelists is ludicrous. And so is thinking that in a city of several million people, I will be lucky enough to bump into Paul Auster and ask him, 'Excuse me, Mr. Auster, would you be so kind as to give me a few minutes of your time?' And if you think this aspect of my plan is lacking in rigour, what will you say about the other part where, once the stars have all aligned, Paul Auster agrees to talk to me, to read my manuscript and to write a foreword! And all of this within a few days so I can come back and say to my wife, 'You'll never guess who I met in New York!' My plan gives new meaning to Paul Auster's novel: going to Brooklyn is pure folly!"

"Indeed," says Dora, relieved.

"Listen, Dora, at the end of *The Trial*, when everything seems lost, Kafka writes this sublime sentence: 'Logic may be unshakeable but it cannot withstand a man who is determined to live.' Well, Dora, I want to live. Do you?"

A few moments before, Dora was wondering whether she should be done with life once and for all. While looking at the river, she flirted with the thought of taking a few more steps – then all her problems would be resolved. In other words, she almost concluded that she didn't want to live anymore. And now this man, this stranger, is asking the question point-blank: do you want to live? Is this a coincidence or the result of a divine machination that is as mean-spirited as it is unlikely? Did this God, in whom she hasn't believed in fifteen years, suddenly decide to make Himself known? Did He, as in that story from her childhood, put a stranger in her path the same way He put an angel in the path of the Virgin Mary? Is this the only way: to wait until the person is on the edge of the abyss, seconds away from making a fatal decision, and say, "Hey! I'm here!" from the top of that ridiculous capital letter? Where was He all those years? Wasn't He paying attention when she was being called a "peasant" and a "wretch" at school? Was He looking the other way when her brother raped her that Christmas night while her parents were at midnight Mass, kneeling before the Father Almighty? Where the hell was He all those years?

The car idles a few yards from an old billboard that reads: Sa 's . The *m* fell off some years ago and no one bothered to replace it. Dora's cousin Michel found the letter the following spring while looking for empty bottles along the road. He dragged it for six miles and then put it up in his bedroom. Dora stares at the missing *m* and wonders whether she wants to live. She wonders if, like this pathetic *m*-less billboard, she too might have lost something along the way. She likes to believe she still has her dignity, but what about self-esteem? What about self-confidence, which is supposedly the key to happiness? Did she forget to replace a letter that fell after a lover's quarrel or a family storm? *A* as in "ambition"? *B* as in "bravery"? *C* as in "courage"? "An entire alphabet is missing," she thinks as her eyes well up with tears. An alphabet of disappointment and despair.

At the moment, she has no boyfriend and few friends. Her friends – invariably the friends of her man of the moment – disappear as soon as the relationship ends.

Even worse, her hobbies are her lovers' hobbies: bowling with Robert, the outdoors with Gaston, jazz with Bill. When they left, those men remained who they were and kept their habits. Robert probably found another bowling partner; Gaston continues to explore the boreal forest without her; and Bill enjoys jazz with his eyes shut, a glass of Courvoisier in his hand. But what about her? What has she kept from those relationships? A few clothes offered as a gift during an outing in Charlevoix. A few Miles Davis albums she doesn't listen to because they invariably bring back bitter memories. Nothing she experienced belongs to her. Nothing she was with those men is part of her.

Her eyes leave the missing *m* and lie on the manuscript again. This stranger, this Max – if that's his real name – has "a thing" that's entirely his own. A lifesaver. A novel he's been writing and rewriting for years. Like her, he must have gone through hard times, but he held on to one very specific thing: a manuscript. Who knows what he must have sacrificed to keep his dream alive. She has no doubt his current strategy will fail. He won't meet Paul Auster. He won't get a foreword for his manuscript and he'll have to rework it again before sending it to a publisher for the umpteenth time. In a few days, they'll be back to square one. Max with his family, she at the restaurant.

She is about to say that she can't abandon her mother and her job, that she doesn't know him and that this adventure is too crazy, when a car appears. The driver slows down, peers inside the car and then keeps going. After a few yards, he makes a right and parks under the *m*-less billboard. Dora didn't recognize the man but she suspects he recognized her. He will show up at Sam's in a few minutes and announce to everybody, "Guys, you'll never guess what our little Dora does before her shift!" Or something along those lines. When she goes in, all eyes will be on her.

Those men, on whom she waits with a smile day in and day out, will chuckle and wink knowingly. Before she finishes tying her apron, one of them will have said something horrible. For them, it will only be teasing. For her, it will be one more insult. She doesn't know who will take the lead – probably one of her favourites who will feel entitled to cross the line because of his status. It is also possible that her cousin Michel, having dragged himself out of bed in time to go to work, will take on the role of public insulter. Everything is possible.

"Listen, Max, I don't have a penny on me. I have no change of clothes. I'm going to lose my job and drive my mother to despair if I don't get out of this car."

Max waits for a moment. Seeing Dora make no attempt to get out, he starts the car and slowly presses the gas pedal. He drives at a crawling pace for a few seconds, then stops. Dora says nothing. She does nothing. She is staring straight ahead. He lifts his foot off the brake and gradually accelerates. Dora watches the trees go by faster and faster. The ones closest to the road soon turn into an uninterrupted curtain of greens and oranges. She closes her eyes for a few seconds. When she opens them again, she sees, reflected in the window, tears streaming down her face. She feels free.

For several long minutes, the two passengers are

silent. The American car swallows the pavement with a familiar and reassuring hum. Every day, millions, indeed tens of millions, of Americans confine themselves in these machines. Some live in them for several hours a day, eating meals or sleeping between meetings. Lovers kiss for the first time, leaning against the door, a few steps from the family house. Children are born on the seats, dead bodies are found in the trunks. Young adults, on their way to their first interview, rehearse their upcoming performance. How many die a violent death, victims of a momentary lapse of attention or a fatal manoeuvre? Clearly, one can live an entire life in a car. And here is Dora, at twenty-seven, linking her destiny to a man in a car on its way to an improbable meeting with Paul Auster.

Some drivers escape to green open spaces; others, like Max and Dora, aim for big cities. Seen from the air, the Ford's trajectory seems perfectly logical. If one were to follow the path carved out of the forest, the car would indeed arrive in New York. Presently, Max drives as if he were fighting a terrible snowstorm. Leaning forward, with both hands on the steering wheel, he appears nervous. As for Dora, she let go of the door handle a few seconds ago. She seems to have convinced herself of the trustworthiness of this expedition. The first to break the silence, she says, "This manuscript that Paul Auster is going to love ... What is it about?"

Max takes a deep breath, relieved. He relaxes in his seat.

"It's a pretty simple story. The story of a hat."

"A hat?"

◀▶

For the next hour, Max recounts the adventures of a poor man, a clerk or an accountant – the story doesn't specify, but implies that his work is dull and repetitive. One day, the man goes in search of a hat that once belonged to Czech writer Franz Kafka. The story is sometimes dark, sometimes slapstick funny. When Max pauses to ask Dora whether she wants to stop for breakfast, P. and the woman from the elevator have just come out of the building. Because Max wants to get to New York before dark, the two travellers waste no time at the table. Back in the car, Dora says, "What happens once they're out of the Old Port building?"

Once they are out, the fireman who accompanied P. hands him over to a policeman. The policeman turns towards the building and, encouraging a somewhat reluctant P. to do the same, says, "Let's wait for your friend."

His "friend"! P. would never have met this hat thief if he hadn't been misled into thinking that opening the stairway door would set off an alarm. He would have simply used the stairs and would be, as we speak, on his way to his apartment, the hat safely resting on his lap.

He pictures the meeting in which a Director of Security casually said, "If we want to restrict access to the stairs, all we have to do is put up a warning such as: Warning! Opening These Doors Will Set Off an Alarm!" They must have had a good laugh before they agreed to the deceitful suggestion! Everything goes behind closed doors. One can discuss stairs and Suitcase Rooms as if nothing matters. One can create fictitious warnings without consideration to how such warnings can end the career of an honest man. P. is more and more angry about this mean, bureaucratic lie. He couldn't get worked up about a faulty elevator – a mechanical contraption devoid of any consciousness – but now that he can sink his teeth into human dishonesty, he is doing it to his heart's content. How could they have been so careless? So irresponsible?

"There she is," says the policeman, waving his colleague over.

The woman responds to the policeman's gesture by waving Kafka's hat above her head. She is all smiles, like a kid about to show a perfect report card to her parents. She walks pressed against the fireman, as if he were walking a bride down the aisle. P. doesn't know why this image of a father and daughter on her wedding day crossed his mind but, confused, he shakes his head as if to erase it. It is, of course, too late. In less time than it takes to say, "I love you," P. has fallen in love. He shakes his head a second time, but nothing will do. The idea of love has slipped into his brain like a file put away for good because the case is closed.

It's ridiculous. P. can't say, "This woman and I have nothing in common," because, to do that, he would first have to know her. But he knows nothing about her. He can't deny that she's pretty, but physical attraction, in and of itself, cannot explain this sudden passion. As the policeman holds his sleeve, and the woman who stole the hat – previously stolen by him – approaches, P. feels a sort of shiver rise inside him. He feels his heart ache. Yes, he really feels something. An inexplicable sensation, but so tangible that we sometimes use the term "lovestruck" to describe it. The idea of love, transformed into a physical sensation, has become real. From then on, P. can accept its existence, evaluate its impact, manage its development, and plan the next steps. When the woman with whom he has just fallen in love gets within a few feet, P. has to fight the intense desire to take out his notebook.

"What an adventure!" exclaims the woman.

"We'll have to ask you to accompany us to the police station."

"The police station!" exclaims P. despite himself.

"It's a formality. I'm sure you can understand that, in the present circumstances, we can't break the Rules."

P., usually mindful of what the Rules – whatever they may be – require, suddenly feels the Rules are overly restrictive. The policeman could have looked the other way and let them go. Without knowing exactly what the Rules say about two people stuck in an elevator, P. finds the blind application of the Rules unfair. Because, let's be honest: the harsh application of a rule, however fair, can lead to injustice.

Let's take P.'s case. He wanted nothing more than to follow the procedures and administrative steps that would lead him to take possession of the hat. He was willing to provide all the necessary paperwork, to answer all the questions and to satisfy all the bureaucratic requirements. He agreed to fetch the hat in good faith and in a spirit of professionalism. But on top of an elevator's mechanical failure and the arrogance of a supervisor in elevator management, he had to contend with less-than-rigorous policies. On top of a security guard's heart failure, he was lied to by the authorities about the use of the stairs. The point here is not to blame the necessarily imperfect nature of a mechanical object or to complain about the ephemeral quality of the human body. Any good manager must contend with such unpredictable attributes, inherent to any business. Disruptions that procedures cannot anticipate (unexpected elevator malfunction or the limitations of the human heart) require the exercise of sound judgment.

"I've never been to a New York police station! Have you?" says the woman.

"Uh, no. I've never been," mumbles P.

The policeman opens the back door of the car, and the woman, taking off the hat she had put back on her head, climbs in like a little girl entering her grandmother's forbidden attic. P. tries to follow, but the policeman closes the door.

"We're not going together?"

"No, you're coming with me," replies the second policeman.

"But there's room for two!"

"Yes, but since we both have to go back to the station, it'll be better this way."

"But ..."

The car with the woman starts before P. has time to voice his objection. Realizing that he risks losing sight of her and, God forbid, never getting the hat back, P. follows the policeman and sits in the back of his cruiser. From his seat, he can follow the woman, thanks to the flashing lights on top of the first car. From time to time, the car in front speeds up and makes a left or a right turn. For a few seconds, P. loses track of it and becomes very tense until his own policeman catches up. For a reason he cannot comprehend, the lights on top of his own car are not on. Is it normal protocol, or did his policeman forget to switch them on? P. doesn't know but, pushing the analysis further, he wonders whether there is a difference in status between him and the woman. Suddenly, his policeman slows down and pulls onto the sidewalk to let two other police cars with flashing lights go by.

A few seconds later, after his policeman has caught up with his colleagues again, P. realizes with terror that he doesn't know which one of the three cars is carrying his hat and the woman he loves. Like kids playing leapfrog, the three cars are constantly changing position. P. sometimes thinks he sees Kafka's hat twirl on the woman's finger, but he loses sight of it again at the next intersection. He abandons the idea of following the progression of the hat, slumps into the seat and takes out his notebook.

He is about to turn the page when he reads: Operation Cadaver. P. glances at the policeman, as if he could have heard what P. just read. He closes both the notebook and his eyes. In a few minutes, he'll be at the police station. The policemen will ask all kinds of questions and might even insist that he empty his pockets. And what will they find? A notebook in which P. explores different ways of getting rid of a dead body. Nothing less. Any reasonable man would consider that proof of guilt. Proof that could only be refuted after an autopsy. After all the damage was done and his career ruined.

If only he had used his notebook like a personal diary! He could have recorded "everything" that happened and noted his impressions at the same time he was describing his actions or strategies – first when the elevator broke down, then when he found the old man's body and, last, when he came to the conclusion that he needed to hide the body. An honest policeman would understand the situation. Worst-case scenario, P. would be accused of lack of judgment in his decision to stuff the security guard in a hockey bag. However, the fragments of information in his notebook are now playing against him.

A horrible thought crosses his mind. Up until now, he has subscribed to the hypothesis of a natural death. Indeed, there was no reason to believe that the poor man had died a violent death. And in the eventuality of a murder accusation, he assumed the autopsy would confirm it was a heart attack or a ruptured aneurysm. And P. would be released.

He now finds it irresponsible to have rejected the hypothesis of murder. What if a crook trying to get hold of a suitcase that wasn't his, or for which he didn't have the right ticket stub, strangled the security guard? Or what if an unscrupulous colleague simply assassinated the old man in order to boost his own career? P. knows nothing about the world of security guards, but he assumes that, like any profession, it comes with its share of jealousy and thwarted hopes, envy and resentment. Or – we've seen worse in the papers – it could be that a serial killer, whose specialty is to murder sexagenarians, is responsible for the poor man's death.

"We're here!"

P. is startled. He had failed to notice that the car has stopped, and the policeman has opened the door. He slips the notebook in his jacket pocket, grabs his hat and the manuscript, and climbs out of the car. No sign of the woman.

"Where is the – my friend?"

"She must be inside. Come, it shouldn't take long. It's a simple formality."

A formality! "Come off it," thinks P. He follows the policeman, all the while wondering how to get rid of his notebook, which has become a terribly incriminating piece of evidence. He could ask to go to the bathroom, throw the notebook in the bowl and flush. That would take care of the problem. Or he could eat the incriminating document. Or he could simply drop it in the nearest trash can; it's unlikely policemen search their own trash every time a crime is committed!

At the end of a long hallway, the policeman opens a door and invites P. to go in. P. enters. The room, which has a single window covered with a white blind, is a rectangle devoid of furniture, except for a bulletin board pinned with a few pieces of paper. There is no table and no chairs. It could almost serve as a broom closet, a small storage room or a locker room except there are no coat hangers, no shelves and no drawers. The room is completely bare and P. cannot guess what it might be used for.

"I'm sorry I can't offer you a chair," says the policeman as he shuts the door.

With the door closed, the room, which seemed small a few seconds ago, becomes minuscule. P. and the policeman stand shoulder to shoulder, facing the window with the white blind. Neither says a word. P. would like to move to the right, but the shoulder that is not pressing against the policeman's shoulder is pressing against the wall. He could back up a few inches, but that would accomplish nothing and, on top of it, he would run the risk of knocking the bulletin board off the wall.

"In any case, it shouldn't be very long."

"..."

"A few minutes at the most," adds the policeman.

"What are we waiting for exactly?" asks P.

"That's always the question, isn't it?"

"..."

"For my colleague to be done with your girlfriend. They're right there, on the other side."

"The other side of what?"

"The mirror, of course."

P. realizes that the woman from the elevator is just a few inches away, probably sitting facing the policeman who escorted her to the police station. He also realizes that the blind is not covering a window to the outside, but a two-way mirror through which people on this side can watch people on the other side without their realizing it. If he pulls up the blind, P. will see the woman without her being able to see him. There is probably a way to activate a system that would allow them to hear the woman's deposition but, evidently, it is not on. P. takes a deep breath and looks up at the ceiling, as if searching for an elevator's model number. There is nothing written on the ceiling, but he is proud to have had the reflex nonetheless. You never know.

"You can take off your hat and your jacket," says the policeman.

Like earlier in the elevator, P. is sweating profusely. He takes off his hat, but has no place to hang it or put it down. He grabs the brim between his teeth and, after slipping the envelope with the manuscript between his legs, he tries to take off his jacket. Every movement causes him to either hit the policeman with his elbow, the bulletin board with his shoulder or the white blind with his head.

"Give me that," says the policeman, taking P.'s hat.

P., his jacket half-off, looks at his hat and then at the policeman. The policeman smiles. "Why do they all want my hats?" wonders P. The policeman leans forward, extends his arm in front of P. and pulls on the cord operating the blind. The blind comes up unevenly, one side at a time. The policeman quietly curses the building and explains to P. that he has to pull up the blind a little at a time, because the cord is not the right length. Every time P. feels the blind is about to go all the way up, he hears a click. The policeman then lowers it by several inches and starts over. For several seconds, P. watches the blind go up and down, and the woman appear and disappear. He is dying to reach for the cord and raise the blind all at once, but he knows such forceful behaviour wouldn't help his cause.

When the blind is finally all the way up, P. can see the woman and the detective. As he expected, they are unaware of his and the policeman's presence. The woman and the detective are not in the classic interrogation position – facing each other, on either side of a table – but are comfortably seated on a couch next to a low table with two cups of coffee and a few cookies. A closed notebook sits on the policeman's lap. The woman is speaking fast and gesticulating with one hand while her other hand strokes the hat nestled on her lap like an affectionate pet. She smiles. From time to time, she and the detective burst out laughing, then take a sip of coffee and start all over again. So much so that the policeman has to lend her his handkerchief so she can wipe the tears of laughter streaming down her cheeks.

What is she talking about? How easy it was to retrieve the hat stolen minutes earlier? How she managed to jump in the elevator just as the doors were closing? Maybe they burst out laughing when she added that P. himself held the elevator doors, allowing her to retrieve the hat like a fruit ripe for the plucking. After several minutes watching them and trying unsuccessfully to read their lips, P. turns to the policeman, "Excuse me, officer, is there a bathroom nearby? I don't feel so good."

"Of course," replies the policeman. "I should have guessed that after all this time in the elevator nature would reassert itself. I'm sorry I didn't offer it to you sooner. Follow me."

The policeman opens the door and takes a step back, forcing P. to turn his head to the right to prevent his nose from being crushed by the man's shoulder blade. For a brief moment, his head turned towards the window, trapped between the policeman and the wall, P. looks at the woman he loves. He imagines strolling along the river or a busy street, walking hand in hand, making small talk, their heads longing for the other's shoulder, laughing at those who are not laughing, not understanding their happiness doesn't encompass the whole world. Walking, walking without ever stopping. Going from movie theatres to restaurants, from bookstores to parks, and living, in the eyes of everybody, in perfect happiness.

"Are you coming?"

The policeman gestures for P. to get out of the room the way a master would ask his dog to bring back the stick it is stubbornly holding in its jaws. A few steps from the interrogation room anteroom, the policeman points to a door. P. slowly turns the knob and, like a man who has bet everything and is leaving it all to luck, enters the bathroom. He quietly closes the door before he can find the light switch so, for a moment, he is embraced by darkness. After a minute or two, he fumbles around for the switch and flips on the light.

P. goes to the sink and sticks his hands under the faucet. After splashing water on his face, he glances in the mirror. A stranger stares back at him with a tired look on his face. He is still without his tie and his eyes, red from anxiety and exhaustion, are blinking repeatedly. Like eyes that cannot remember what they have seen. Or eyes that have seen too much and are struggling to erase the images they have unwittingly captured. Eyes that cannot believe their eyes. He looks around for a towel but, unable to find one, slumps down on the toilet.

His hand angles towards his jacket's inside pocket, where his notebook is stored but, suddenly, instead of slipping between the jacket and the white shirt, it makes a beeline for the yellow envelope. P. pulls out the manuscript, opens it randomly and starts reading a short story titled "I Lost My Calvino."

I Lost My Calvino

The detective looked me in the eye and repeated what I had just told him. Actually, it would be more accurate to write: the detective looked me in the eye and repeated what I had just told him but changed the personal pronoun, the possessive pronoun and the verb's person: "You lost your Calvino." To make sure there was no ambiguity in the affair, I, in turn, flipped the terms of what had become his sentence and, re-appropriating it, confirmed: "That's right. I lost my Calvino." The detective, who probably knew from experience that one cannot repeat the same sentence indefinitely without draining it of meaning, looked down and wrote in his notebook, "The individual claims he lost his Calvino."

I was flabbergasted. How could a sentence so simple, so descriptive – a sentence that left so little open to interpretation – go, within seconds, from the realm of certainty to the realm of opinion? How could an honest man of law, whose role was no more and no less than to report facts the way they were presented to him, engage in such an exercise in hermeneutics? Because we should not think that the mistake is without consequence:

a man who states something does not claim anything.

I confronted him on the spot. "I'm sorry, detective. I'm not claiming I lost my Calvino; I actually lost it. I hope you can appreciate the nuance."

The detective looked at me with a tired expression on his face, leaned over his notebook and started writing again, this time making sure I couldn't see. After a few seconds, he closed his notebook, looked up, smiled faintly and said, "Follow me."

At the end of the hallway, the detective opened a door and showed me into a small room. It was a square and stark room with a table and three chairs. The light was dim and the walls completely white. The scene reminded me of those American movies where corrupt policemen rough up gangsters whose guilt they take as a given. I was wondering what kind of questions a detective who wants to know where my Calvino was might ask when I heard the door slam shut.

A man came towards me, put his jacket on one of the three chairs but kept his hat on – one of those ridiculous little fedoras that no one wears anymore. Without introducing himself, he asked in a monotone voice, "When did you last see your Calvino?" I stood up and extended my hand but, before I could introduce myself, he cut me off and said with irritation, "Enough with the formalities. I'm a busy man. I know who you are and why you're here. You're the twelfth person to have lost a Calvino this week. I have no time to lose." He then repeated the question. Actually, he repeated the same words but changed the tone. His question, purely descriptive the first time, now implied that he was sick of idiots incapable of looking after their Calvinos, that he had no time to waste and that his own Calvino was safe and sound: "When did you last see your Calvino?"

Though I listened until the end, my mind stopped – maybe because of my interest in numbers – at this rather surprising sentence: "You're the twelfth person to have lost a Calvino this week." Whether, in a single day, several people around the world can lose a book or have a book stolen is, from a theoretical standpoint, highly probable and, from a statistical standpoint, easily demonstrable. I, myself, have lost several books throughout the years. Between this Calvino and the ones that were stolen, the ones I lost, the ones I destroyed accidentally, the ones I lent and never got back, the ones I had to abandon with old girlfriends, the ones my mother threw out because she deemed them immoral, I can affirm that the number falls between forty and sixty.

Obviously, what I just said has no scientific value. If I had to estimate annual Calvino losses,

I would rely on proven data collection methods, not personal anecdotes. For example, I would first determine how many Calvinos are in circulation throughout the world. Publishing houses have, in the past, been amenable to this kind of study, and nothing leads me to believe it would be any different for Calvino. Second, it would be useful to map those Calvinos by country or, when appropriate, by region, and to calculate their growth rate. Next, I could survey Calvino owners to get a sense of the number of reported losses. This data could then be compared to reports from different police stations, those representing more or less the official list of Calvino losses recorded annually. In my opinion, such a study would not only set the record straight in terms of actual Calvino losses, but it might lead to the adoption of legislative measures aiming to end a situation that has become intolerable.

Once I was done with this scenario, I remembered how I came to elaborate it and resumed, so to speak, my train of thought: "You're the twelfth person to have lost a Calvino this week." Granted, a man can lose forty books throughout the course of his life. But to have twelve people, in a city of fewer than three hundred thousand people, lose a book written by the same author within a few days, is beyond comprehension. While a part of my brain was busy formulating an answer to the question of the man towering over me, another part of that same brain was trying to explain what we call in our profession "a statistical anomaly."

Why such a high number of lost Calvinos? Familiar with this kind of exercise, I started elaborating working hypotheses. A Calvino conference at the university? All my colleagues know my interest in this author, so I would have been informed. A film adaptation of a Calvino story, which led to an infatuation for the work of the Italian novelist and caused everybody to walk around with his book under their arm? Again, I read the paper every day and such news wouldn't have escaped me. I was about to formulate a third hypothesis when a fist brutally landed on the table: "When did you last see your Calvino?"

I instinctively sank deeper into my chair. I also noted that, within seconds, the question had taken on a third meaning. The indifference of the first version and the condescension of the second had been replaced by a disturbing verbal violence. Stunned by this sudden turn of events and by the aggressiveness of the question, I decided to reply tit for tat but without, however, going beyond the parameters of the questions: "I last saw my Calvino three days ago, on April 12, 2007, at 9:55 p.m."

I was well aware that though his question referred to a specific aspect of my Calvino's disappearance (the temporal aspect), it was really "fishing" for

> a broader answer. Implied in the question were many more questions which, although implicit, should have led me to contextualize the disappearance of the book and establish a cause-and-effect relationship between the different ideas. On second thought, the exact time of the book's disappearance was not useful to the investigation. But I thought, "If this man is incapable of tact when dealing with innocent victims, I don't see why I should make his job easy by expanding beyond the facts."
>
> I expected him to accuse me of trying to be smart, but he straightened up and said, obviously pleased, "I see you've decided to co-operate."
>
> "Co-operate!" I repeated, incredulous. "What's going on here? I lost a book. And although, I admit it, it's not the end of the world, I feel it's important to report it, out of public-spiritedness and so annual statistics about lost objects are not skewed."
>
> The man lit a cigarette (one would have believed it was 1940) and opened a briefcase. He consulted it for a few seconds then, nonchalantly closing it, said the following line: "We don't believe a word of your story, Mr. Martin."

P. closes the manuscript. For several long minutes, he remains seated on the toilet, motionless, disconcerted by the unreal yet terribly pertinent nature of this story.

Why is he taking the time to read excerpts from this manuscript? He has always denigrated people who waste their time reading fiction, but all of a sudden, he feels connected to these seemingly inconsequential stories. These strange stories, which didn't seem to amount to much at first, are slowly changing his way of thinking. Even though they don't relate to him, he feels they put distance between him and the world.

"Are you okay?" asks the policeman.

"Yes, just a minute."

P. needs to get rid of the notebook. He also needs to figure out how to retrieve his two hats, get out of the police station and go home. Once he gets to his place, there'll be no time to lose. He'll have to pack his suitcase and leave the city. He could, of course, rent a dingy apartment somewhere downtown, but the prospect of living in that neighbourhood doesn't appeal to him. All things considered, he would rather leave and negotiate the terms of the ransom from a distance. Being naturally frugal, P.'s bank account is relatively fat. He'll take a shower, eat a sandwich, pack his suitcase and, within a few hours, be aboard the first train out of town.

Beforehand, he'll withdraw all of his savings. P. knows he has exactly $3,455.14 in his bank account. If he manages this little nest egg in a smart and efficient way, he can live worry-free for several weeks. He can take his time, find an apartment in a small university town and pretend he's teaching accounting at the local college. He could also make up a story harder to verify; for example, he's writing a thesis and has decided to exile himself to have some quiet time. Or, he's a writer and wants to put the final touch on his latest book. A book about hats and dead writers' ghosts. A book with a tragic ending.

In any case, he can't go back to the Midwest because someone is bound to recognize him. The Boss will probably offer a generous ransom for his capture and there'll be no shortage of old acquaintances willing to turn him in to the police. Money, the ultimate value in this country, easily displaces friendship.

"Are you okay?" asks the policeman on the other side of the door.

"Yes, just a minute. I'm coming."

P. takes out his notebook and scans the room. The options are few: the trash can, the sink or the toilet bowl. Or his stomach, of course. The best option would be to burn the incriminating evidence but, in a room this small, it wouldn't be hard to figure out who lit the fire. Plus, P. is not a smoker; he has no matches or lighter on him. If he chooses the trash can, he has to tear up the notebook. But a dedicated policeman could put the pages back together. And his fingerprints might still be "readable." He could tear up half the pages and swallow the other half – that would make it impossible to reconstruct the notebook. But P. doesn't feel particularly well. He would rather not ingest paper. He might throw up before his gastric acid has erased the damning sentences. Which leaves the sink or the toilet bowl. He is weighing the pros and cons of both options when the policeman knocks on the door.

"Come on, we have to go. Your friend is waiting for you," urges the policeman.

The woman from the elevator has finished her

deposition. P. jumps to his feet, lifts the toilet seat and throws the notebook in the bowl.

"I'm coming!"

He flushes and waits. The bowl fills up normally. He waits a little longer. To his horror, the toilet overflows – spilling water all over the floor – and his notebook comes back from its brief stay in the pipes of the police station. P. takes off his jacket, rolls up his shirt sleeve and sticks his arm in the bowl. He grabs the notebook. Just as he is about to implement the "sink" scenario, he hears a key in the lock. He slips the soaked notebook in his jacket pocket. When the policeman opens the door, P. is putting the toilet seat down.

The policeman sees water on the floor and turns to P., who fears the policeman will immediately figure out that he tried to get rid of the incriminating evidence. He will handcuff him in a flash and walk him to the interrogation room *manu militari*. Then they will search him and find the notebook. If P. is lucky, the ink will have bled and the pages will be unreadable. But he has no doubt the police will want to know why he tried to flush his notebook down the toilet.

"I'm so sorry, this damn toilet played its trick on you! Don't worry, it happens all the time. Come."

The two men walk by the room where, a few minutes earlier, the woman and the detective were trading funny stories and stuffing themselves with cookies. The room is empty.

"You're not taking my deposition?"

"It won't be necessary. Your friend gave us all the information we needed. My colleague will take you back."

P. can hardly believe it. They're going to let them go! Outside, the woman smiles and invites him to climb in the police car with her. Just as P. is about to step in, the policeman screams, "Wait!"

P. freezes and looks at the woman, perhaps intending to tell her that he loves her but that, unfortunately, fate doesn't always co-operate; that the policeman noticed something; that they are going to take him away ... In a word, the same dark scenario P. imagines every time he feels liberated.

"You forgot your hat!"

P. turns around and, one foot on the concrete, the other in the car, caught between freedom and oppression, between yesterday and today, he takes his hat as if it were a gift from the heavens. In the car, the policeman asks the two passengers, "Where can I drop you off?"

The woman looks into P.'s eyes and, addressing the policeman, says, "My car is right by the Old Port building, if you don't mind."

"No problem. And, sir?"

"He's with me," answers the woman, handing Kafka's hat to P.

Since Max has interrupted his story, Dora asks, "And then?"

And then, Max tells her, another story begins. The story of a man and woman learning to know each other on the roads of America. Also the story of an improbable but catastrophic meeting between reality and fiction. But to finish the New York episode, let's say that P. and the woman from the elevator are silent while the policeman drives them to the port.

P. watches people and shop windows go by. He tells himself that the worst is over. He retrieved his hat. He got out of "that damn building" – as he is now in the habit of calling it – alive. He left the police station unharmed. In a few minutes, the policeman will open the door and wish him a good day.

"Here we are."

P. looks at the woman. She smiles. Although he has made up his mind and drawn his plan, he feels the woman's presence jeopardizes the success of the operation. She gave him back the hat, but she is still holding a part of him, now and forever. Who knows, maybe he owes her his freedom. Without her, the policemen would have taken his deposition. What would they have asked? "What were you doing in the elevator? Who in the building were you there to see? Why do you have two hats?" P. might have snapped. He might have unwittingly revealed a fact that, for a seasoned policeman, would have proved crucial. He might have slipped and talked about the Suitcase Room or the fire in the Hat Room. If such a room exists! Yes, the more he thinks about it, the more he feels this woman saved his life and he owes her everything.

P. and the woman walk side by side for a moment. The sidewalk is crowded and the street full of tourists. A few steps from where the woman parked her car earlier that day, P. notices two men sitting on a park bench. Two twins dressed identically and, as if this were not ridiculous enough for middle-aged men, reading identical books.

"Can I drop you somewhere?"

"Uh … I don't think so. I think that –"

"You lied to me, right?"

"Lied?"

"In the elevator."

"In the elevator?"

"It wasn't your first time. You've gotten stuck before."

"I –"

"It's okay. I understand."

"It's just that, you see, I had a gruelling day."

3

The man at the wheel of the American sedan cannot be more than forty. Although soberly dressed, he seems ill at ease in the formal clothes – black jacket, white shirt, dark tie – he picked for the trip. The car is spacious but, from time to time, between manoeuvres, his head hits the ceiling and his hat – small and round – falls over his eyes or one of his ears. He swiftly and meticulously adjusts it. Black and alert, his eyes – like the eyes of a small rodent – constantly move between the road and the rear-view mirror. From time to time, he looks over his left shoulder. He is driving in silence.

In fact, the other two passengers, considerably more talkative than he is, make it impossible for him to get a word in. Comfortably seated in the back seat, they chat about everything and nothing. Before leaving New York, when it came time to decide who would drive, the man with the hat said as a joke that he would be honoured to drive such great men – he was already dressed for the job anyway. As they prepared to leave, he opened the door and invited his companions to be seated in the luxury car rented for the occasion. When his illustrious clients filed past, he touched his hat with the tips of his fingers and leaned slightly forward as a mark of deference. All three are professional writers.

Sitting behind the driver, a small, elderly man plays with a wooden cane – an ageless, twisted stick that probably belonged to his father – twirling it around and around in his bony hands. The old man's head is like a planet with blurry edges and undiscovered riches. His shiny hair, which time has not managed to steal, ripples majestically on the back of his head before plunging down his neck, like a stupendous waterfall from the Amazon. Leaning slightly to the right, he listens to his travelling companion with his eyes closed. He is blind.

The third and last passenger, taller and younger than the blind man but older than the "driver," wears elegant clothes and fine leather shoes. Before sitting down, he placed his Panama hat on the seat next to the driver. A seat, as we know, that is unoccupied. His penetrating eyes, which could be qualified as intelligent, rest sometimes on one of his fellow passengers, sometimes on the scenery outside. He is twirling a fountain pen between his long, agile fingers and seems on the lookout for any gesture, phrase or object worth capturing as descriptive imagery in the notebook open on his lap. He is Italian.

Our three characters left New York a few hours ago and are on their way to Montreal, where organizers and attendees of an international conference titled The Writer As Character are waiting for them. The driver with the hat, the blind man and the Italian are the conference's guests of honour and, as such, will take turns explaining their theories on the writer-character relationship. They will share the stage during the opening ceremony, meet with the media, talk with writers from every continent and, for three days, be treated like royalty. The Prime Minister, not usually inclined to mix with artists, might even meet with them privately.

The blind man has prepared a dense and sometimes abstruse speech in which he talks about the infinite nature of the imagination and postulates that there is no fundamental difference between a writer and a character. He will tell the story of a writer who, in one of his own stories, randomly bumps into an older version of himself sitting on a park bench. Faithful to his style of argumentation, this made-up story will become the irrefutable proof of his theory. He might also cite a few fictitious authors with unpronounceable names, whose authority would never be questioned by those who have idolized him for so many years.

The Italian, for his part, will trace the evolution of intertextuality since Homer and analyze the writer-character dichotomy through the lens of that literary theory. He will provide an exhaustive list of novels and short stories in which writers appear – whether their own creations or the creations of others. What will emerge from this analysis, both erudite and funny, is a rather seductive interpretation of literature according to which imagination (read: character) and reality (read: writer) work hand in hand in creating the work – something he cannot say without a certain emotion.

As for the driver with the hat, he has no idea what he is going to say. For now, his only preoccupation is to get to Montreal.

Presently, the Italian says to his two travelling companions, "If you stare straight in front of you, without letting your eyes follow the apparent movement of things, the trees become an uninterrupted curtain whose beginning and end we cannot distinguish. It's almost impossible to see the forest for the trees. Even a most discerning observer, who wouldn't know that this curtain is made of trees, wouldn't figure it out solely based on observation, however pointed. It's as if the individual tree has no beginning or end. Properly speaking, and from our current perspective, the tree doesn't exist. Only the forest is observable."

"You always think everything is a question of perspective!" exclaims the blind man. "You'll never change, you stubborn Italian."

"It's not about perspective, but about our relationship to space-time. Speed is what reduces the tree's specificity, not perspective. We can even say that speed returns the tree to the noble and universal principle of the forest, without which its existence is as banal as it is ridiculous. A tree, like a human being, doesn't amount to much without the reassuring and abundant presence of its peers. If our good driver here could go even faster, the entire forest would disappear without our having changed perspective at all. If he ignored the fundamental principles of physics altogether, and pushed the car to a speed to this day unimaginable, the entire horizon would disappear."

"And why not the universe?"

"Indeed, why not the universe?"

The Italian then says to the driver, "I told you to rent a Lamborghini instead of this ridiculous American tank! Aboard this raft, we have no chance of bringing to conclusion the experiment suggested by our friend."

The driver adjusts his hat and smiles.

"They always think too big or too small," he reflects. "For them, life only makes sense insofar as it can be broken into increasingly smaller, observable parts, or viewed through increasingly larger, universal principles. Life is here, in the countless details of day-to-day experience, in all that is unpredictable and incomprehensible about the very act of living."

The driver looks over his shoulder, getting ready to switch lanes. The traffic being intense, and drivers not being inclined to surrender so much as an inch of what they consider their personal space, he has to attempt the manoeuvre several times. He finally makes it into the left lane, driving at high speed, and adjusts his hat with a shaky hand. A bead of sweat has formed on his upper lip.

"It reminds me of that story about the twin brothers with diametrically opposite perspectives," says the blind man. "Have you heard it? It happened several years ago in a Nordic country ..."

"A Nordic country! Who would have thought? Well, tell us," says the Italian, a smile on his lips.

"Yes, in Norway," adds the blind man, now smiling too. "In any case, the two brothers – Irtha and Bingher – were born on a full moon, on a January 22, to be exact. They were what we call monozygotic twins, meaning they came from a single egg."

"Identical twins, you mean."

"Yes, perfectly identical. I'll spare you the details of their childhood but if you're interested, Karl Openstirboek wrote an interesting biography called, if memory serves, *Irtha & Bingher: An Uncommon Destiny*."

"I'll buy it as soon as I get back to Rome," says the Italian.

The three travellers share a moment of silence tinted with respectful irony. The kind of silence that no words can describe, because it actually celebrates what words leave unsaid. This silence reminds us that words are all we have to describe the world and create it. Everything else is trivial.

Those three men never drove from New York to Montreal together. They are here only to remind us that words can do extraordinary things: they can invent worlds where the dead and the living walk side by side; they can create a character whose traits remind us of an author, himself half-man, half-character; and they can bring writers, who never met in real life, together on the page. Those three men were also brought here to plant doubt in the mind of the reader, who will eventually have to decide what meaning to give to the last scene of this story about hats and extraordinary writers.

To facilitate this undertaking, the reader should immediately take out the notebook in which they write their thoughts, because in a few lines, it might be too late.

They can start a new page and write, at the very top, in capital letters: "POSSIBLE ENDINGS." They can also, if they feel it would structure their thoughts better, write the numerals one to ten in the left margin. The author gives them freedom to organize their thoughts as they please, and to determine the limits of the possible and the impossible, of the real and the fantastic. Although it is true that the author would appreciate a credible ending to the story of the man trying to fetch a hat, and to the story of that other man trying to meet Paul Auster, he nevertheless accepts any conclusion, whether crazy, fantastic or even erotic. As for this last option, however, the author asks for a minimum of restraint, because he is not accustomed to that literary genre. In truth, he would be a little embarrassed if his name were associated with it.

A few moments later, the blind man picks up his train of thought.

"Although from a modest upbringing, Irtha and Bingher attended the best schools of Europe. Studious, serious and ambitious, they graduated first-of-class from their respective programs and eventually taught at the Massachusetts Institute of Technology. We don't know how nature determines these things but, beyond outward appearances, the two brothers were very different. This difference – or 'opposition' even – was documented in great detail in the personal diary of their neighbour, a certain Atlerht, if I'm not mistaken. But I forget her first name."

"Never mind her first name. This name suits her perfectly," adds the Italian. "Even if, like Irtha and Bingher, it doesn't sound typically Norwegian."

"In any case, our identical twins were driven by what Atlerht calls 'opposite impulses,' not a very scientific term, but one that accurately describes our two protagonists."

"Protagonists? This is not based on real life?"

"Of course, but when you tell a story, whether real or imaginary, its actors – or agents, if you prefer – become characters. I'll have a chance to talk about that tomorrow night. Anyway, the first twin, given to outwardness and the exploration of heights, kept climbing on tables, in trees and, later, on the roof of the local church. His brother, on the other hand, preferred depths, the exploration of local caves and scuba diving. He read in the basement while his brother read in the attic."

"Because they both liked reading, of course."

"Indeed," says the blind man, "they loved reading. Their great uncle, an erudite man named Fröberg, once published an important treatise on philology. But I'm straying. To get back to our subject, you will understand that one spent his childhood exploring lake bottoms while the other tried to always go higher. Probably disappointed by the necessarily finite nature of terrestrial heights, he went from rock climbing to aviation before moving on to space exploration.

Irtha became an oceanologist; Bingher, a first-class astronaut. They both had brilliant careers, published papers in the most important scientific journals and spoke at countless conferences. But what's interesting in their story is not so much the antinomic aspect of their personalities – it's their mysterious and tragic ending. The twins disappeared on the same day, a January 22, at the exact age of forty-three. Irtha, aboard a submarine sounding the depths of the ocean; Bingher, aboard a spaceship en route to Mars. A few years later, the shuttle was brought back to Earth and the submarine was recovered off the coast of Sumatra, but the twins' bodies were never found."

"We're not accustomed to so much symmetry from you, my dear friend."

"I'm just summarizing the story."

"Just summarizing! Come on, you know very well that if we gave the same book to a hundred people and asked them to summarize it in three pages, there wouldn't be two identical sentences in those three hundred pages."

"I agree with you," replies the blind man, "because you know my weakness for the charms of infinity. That said, Openstirboek proposes two theories that might explain the twins' strange disappearance. The first theory is that it was pure coincidence. Despite rather convincing clues that it was all premeditated, it's possible it was just an incredible coincidence and neither free will nor destiny played a role. Life is like that. The second explanation will seduce rational beings, especially you, dear young driver. According to this theory, once at the top of their respective fields of study, the twins concluded that it was impossible to understand those fields in their totality. In other words, confronted with the theoretical and practical impossibility of giving meaning to the object of their quest, they decided to make things worse by adding the mystery of their disappearance. Openstirboek postulates that the twins' objective was no less than working out an equation that would explain the complexity of the entire universe. He even adds that their most pressing desire was to distill this complexity to a mathematical figure, or even a single number that would, in and of itself, explain everything."

The blind man turns his closed eyes towards the Italian and asks what he thinks. The Italian watches the trees go by. They are still four hours away from Montreal and he is happy he managed to convince his two colleagues to do the trip by car. He even finds himself dreaming they will never reach their destination, forever doomed to wander the roads of New England, between New York and Montreal.

"Well, if you want my opinion, I think there's a third possibility," says the Italian, interrupting his daydreaming.

"I'd be happy to hear it."

"To me, these two scenarios lack imagination."

"Now, there's a criticism I don't often hear," replies the blind man, feigning indignation.

"No, you certainly don't lack imagination. And anyway, what you shared were Openstirboek's impressions, not yours. But these 'scenarios,' insofar as scenarios can have weaknesses, lack imagination. They're too symmetrical."

"I see," says the blind man.

"In any case, when you were telling the story, I remembered reading something about the two men."

"I was a little surprised to hear that you didn't know them. I feel better," adds the blind man, touching the Italian's left arm with his hand.

"Not only do I know this story, I met a man at the

Paris Book Fair several years ago who claimed to be their distant cousin."

"That's the spirit!"

"We had a strange conversation and, now that you've reminded us of the twins' story, it's all coming back to me."

"Memory is a most creative faculty, don't you think?"

"Indeed, most creative," says the Italian. "He told me a funny story. Apparently, a few days before their death, while they were vacationing in New York City, the twins decided to go book shopping as a way to pass the time. As you previously mentioned, my dear friend, they were from a modest upbringing where literature was omnipresent. But I'll be in a better position to appreciate this part of their lives after I have read Mr. Alpenbucher's book."

"*Openstirboek,* not 'Alpenbucher,'" the blind man points out, all smiles. "Karl Openstirboek."

"Unlike you, I have no memory for names. So anyway, they randomly go into a bookstore and find a book titled *Kafka's Hat.*"

"Just what we needed," proclaims the driver, breaking his silence for the first time.

"There are only two copies of the book and the twins decide to buy them both. They walk for a while and find a park bench by the Customs building."

"The Old Port building?" asks the driver.

"Yes, that one. The two brothers sit on the bench and start reading the story of a strange man who must one day fetch a hat that used to belong to Franz Kafka. But I'll spare you the many adventures of the Stuff & Things Co. employee. What's important here is the man and his girlfriend's mysterious and tragic demise."

"Tragic?" asks the driver.

"Yes," answers the Italian. "They die in a terrible car accident, like thousands of others in this country. After coming out of the police station, the main character, P., confides in the woman he has known only for a few hours. She immediately understands his distress and invites him to go to Vermont, where her parents live. They leave New York in the late afternoon. But what's mysterious in this story, and where the connection to the story of our two Norwegians really starts to make sense, is that, contrary to the depositions of a dozen highly credible witnesses asserting there were three cars involved in the accident, only two cars were ever found.

"All this to say that *Kafka's Hat*, in which three writers disappear without a trace, would be, according to the twins' cousin, the last novel they read before they too disappeared."

The driver abruptly turns to the Italian to ask him a question but, in doing so, knocks his hat on the floor on the passenger's side.

"My hat!" says the driver.

"I see it," says the Italian.

"It's okay, it's okay, don't worry," says the driver.

The Italian tries to grab the hat, but cannot reach it without unbuckling his seat belt. Before he has time to do so, the driver has leaned forward. In the process, he hits the windshield wipers lever, causing the wipers to dance furiously in front of his eyes. Surprised by the abrupt awakening of these plastic and rubber twins, he unintentionally swerves to the left. Absorbed by the Italian's story, the driver had considerably slowed down.

So much so that the driver in the car that has been following them for several miles is getting impatient, and is looking for the right moment to pass this "raft," to use the Italian's expression.

There are only two passengers in the car behind the writers' sedan. A woman, as we said before, and a small man with two hats nestled into one another, and a thick yellow envelope on his lap. The driver of the sedan swerves just as the woman finally decides to pass. If it hadn't been for a third car, coming from the opposite direction, she would have had time to retreat behind the sedan. But unfortunately, the third car was going fast because its occupants – a woman and a man – were determined to make it to New York before dark.

The next morning, a child, attracted by the smoke coming off the cars' charred remains, decided to investigate what was happening at the edge of the family farm. He jumped over the fence and landed on a thick yellow envelope. He looked inside and closed it again. Next, he headed towards the wreckage that had been pushed to the side of the road. After inspecting the chrome and metal remains of the two cars, which the impact had more or less fused into one, he climbed back over the fence. On the way back, he found a small black hat in a ditch. He put it on his head, clutched the yellow envelope against his chest and made his way home, whistling away.

Chantal Bilodeau is a New York–based playwright and translator originally from Montreal. Her play *Sila* won first prize in the 2012 Earth Matters on Stage Ecodrama Festival and the 2011 Uprising National Playwriting Competition. She is the recipient of a Jerome Travel and Study Grant and a National Endowment for the Arts Fellowship. Notable among her English translations are *Bintou* by Koffi Kwahulé and *Abraham Lincoln Goes to the Theatre* by Larry Tremblay.